EVERYONE'S SWEETHEART

A Small Town Murder Mystery

Andi Warden

Latigo Press, LLC

Copyright © 2023 Latigo Press, LLC

All rights reserved

The characters and events portrayed in this book are fictitious. Any similarity to real persons, living or dead, is coincidental and not intended by the author.

No part of this book may be reproduced, or stored in a retrieval system, or transmitted in any form or by any means, electronic, mechanical, photocopying, recording, or otherwise, without express written permission of the publisher.

"But people in a small town tend to do a lot of talking, even when they don't know what they're talking about."

DON ROFF

CONTENTS

Title Page
Copyright
Epigraph
Chapter One   1
Chapter Two   7
Chapter Three   15
Chapter Four   22
Chapter Five   28
Chapter Six   35
Chapter Seven   43
Chapter Eight   50
Chapter Nine   58
Chapter Ten   65
Chapter Eleven   74
Chapter Twelve   80
Chapter Thirteen   88
Chapter Fourteen   95

Chapter Fifteen	102
Chapter Sixteen	108
Chapter Seventeen	115
Epilogue	122
Want more?	127
About The Author	129
Books By This Author	131

CHAPTER ONE

"I'm so incredibly sorry for your loss, Beth." Pastor Frank shook my hand, his grip cold and clammy. "Brad was one of the best men I've ever known—and I mean that. He'd give a man the shirt off his back. It's just tragic what happened. All because of a wasp. Who would've thought?"

Someone who's allergic to them. I held back my offhanded comment, knowing not everyone coped well with my sense of humor.

"Dad was a good man," I replied instead. "Thank you for putting on such a great service for him."

"Anything for your family. Let me know if you need anything. You, too, Andrea," he added, turning to my mom as she held the door for him. He ran his fingers through his white mustache. "You know the church is always here for you."

"Of course, thank you so much. I'll see you Sunday." Mom smiled as he tipped his hat. She shut the front door of the old farmhouse and spun around, resting her back against the door as her face filled with relief. "I am so glad that's over. I know your father was a social man, but my word, I didn't expect the whole town to show up to our house. We were all crammed in here like a bad Black Friday sale at Walmart."

"I don't know why you'd expect anything less—but actually, it wasn't the *whole* town," I pointed out, brushing some of my auburn hair from my eyes. "No one my age showed up." *Thank God.*

"That's only because no one you know knew that you were coming into town, Beth." Mom gave me a side eye as she passed me, heading toward the old, faded dining room table. "And none of the kids your age go to our church anymore anyway, leaving only all of us old folk to know he even passed away. They go to that new one in Gale—the one with the loud music. I swear, they're all living in their own world, and probably sin for that matter. Drugs are everywhere these days."

I nodded but stayed quiet with my commentary. If she only knew that it had been *years* since I'd set foot in any religious establishment—or taken drugs.

Letting out a sigh, I grabbed one of the casserole dish lids and started trying to fit it to one of the many glass pans strewn out on the table.

"We need to make sure we take one or two of these out to Blaze," Mom remarked, her shoulders slumping. "There's no way you and I will eat it all."

"Blaze? Is that the new ranch manager Dad hired?" I racked my brain, trying to remember which one he was at the funeral. I was bad with names and faces—especially in a town I had no desire to be back in.

Rustdale, Texas. The most miserable place on earth.

"He hired Blaze nearly three years ago, honey." Mom gave me a knowing look, her dark eyes flashing with grief. But she didn't expand on the thought, and I was thankful that she avoided chiding me for not coming home in over five years. "Would you mind taking this out to him?" She held out two glass dishes, mostly full of unappealing Southern cuisine. "When you get back, I'll help you finish unpacking."

I took the pans from her as she nodded. "The apartment over the barn, right?"

"Yeah, that's the one. The same one that our ranch manager has always stayed in." Her smile felt a little forced. But I didn't want to go there.

She was grieving the loss of my dad, and so was I. There was no point in starting anything. There was enough pain—and we were all each other had left. That thought alone was enough to make my stomach churn with sadness. There were too many bad memories attached to this town.

Mom opened the front door for me, allowing the humid summer air to encircle me. It was suffocating in early September, my lungs feeling heavy as my boots thudded across the painted white porch. Spending the past five years in Chicago had been less than pleasant, but I didn't miss the Southern heat.

I did miss these cowboy boots, though.

My eyes drifted down to my old boots, a pair of dark

brown custom-made stovetops that my dad had gotten me as a gift my senior year of high school. I'd left them behind when I'd started law school out of state years ago, never thinking I'd need them again.

A pang of regret hit me in the chest. *Maybe I should've come home more.*

Swallowing hard, I pushed the thought away. That was the thing about regret—there's nothing you can do to change it. I might not have been home in years, busy working as a defense attorney in Chicago, but I did call home once or twice a week. My dad knew that I loved him, just as much as he knew being home hurt worse than being gone. I huffed as I climbed the stairs to the apartment, cradling the casserole dishes in my arms. Shifting their weight to the left, I knocked on the old heavy wooden door.

It swung open to a tall, dark-headed, hazel-eyed cowboy looking down at me. "What can I do for you, Beth?"

"These are for you." I held out the pans, surprised he knew who I was—even though I shouldn't have been. I was certain my dad probably talked the poor man's ear off, blabbing about my uptown big-time lawyer job.

And the divorce, too. Yikes.

He eyed the dishes, before stepping aside. "You can sit them on the table."

"Or... you could just take them and not be lazy." I raised an eyebrow, daring him to challenge me.

"You sound just like your old man," he chuckled, though his voice trailed off a little. "It's gonna be really weird without him tellin' me what to do all damn day." His thin lips sank into a deep frown that tugged at my heartstrings.

"Yeah, probably so. He was really good at bossing people around." I held out the pans, still not taking the invite into his apartment as he motioned for me to come in. If there was anything I had learned after becoming a criminal defense attorney, it was to not be dumb.

And going into a strange man's apartment is dumb.

A smirk grew across his face and shaking his head, he took them from my arms. "How long are you planning on staying here in town?"

"I don't know." I shrugged, relaxing a little, though his gaze made my stomach flutter. "I haven't figured that out yet. I know Mom wants me to deal with Greg, the family attorney, on Dad's will. Beyond that, I don't know what I'm doing—but I'm not staying here long term."

"Huh, interesting. You got any reason to go back to the Windy City?" he asked, setting the casserole dishes down on the entryway table and eyeing me. "Because rumor has it that you had to quit your big fancy firm with that hot shot—what's his name? Jared?"

I narrowed my eyes at the name drop. "I guess not everyone likes working with their ex-husband day in and day out. It can be a little..."

"Tense?"

The amusement on his face was irritating. "Uh, yeah. Let's go with that." I let out a sigh. "For someone I've never met, you sure know a lot about me."

He smiled playfully, biting his lower lip. "Your dad was just itching for you to come back here and meet me, ya know. He never cared for that ex-husband of yours. He didn't think he was the right one."

"He made that known more than once—about my ex-husband," I added, leveling with him, a salty smile on my face. "I can't recall him mentioning you though. I never had much of an eye for cowboys. But I won't be around long enough for it to matter anyway." Shrugging, I spun on my heels, heading back down the stairs.

"We'll see," he called after me from the doorway. "I can be pretty hard to leave."

"Oh, I bet," I snorted, rolling my eyes as I made it to the last step. It didn't matter how handsome Blaze was—or if my dad actually thought the two of us would hit it off.

I wasn't here to get involved in anything.

CHAPTER TWO

"So, what did you think of Blaze?" Mom asked me, sipping her coffee as I stepped onto the front porch, a grocery list in my hands.

"I think he's just another cowboy," I quipped, shaking my head, though my eyes drifted out to the corral where he was loping one of the colts. If I were seventeen again, I might've been drooling over the way he made it look so easy—but I wasn't that girl anymore. I learned a long time ago that riding horses would never come naturally to me. I turned back to the paper in my hand. "This is a really long list. I mean, there's still a whole fridge full of casseroles."

She shrugged, her eyes still on Blaze. "I'm tired of eating casserole."

"Mom, the funeral was yesterday."

"I know, but I just don't like casserole." Her eyes came back to meet mine, rimmed with a sadness that was a punch right to the gut.

I gave her a hug around her shoulders, squeezing her. "We can throw them all out if you want."

She laughed, wiping a rogue tear from her cheek.

"That's okay. We'll just keep feeding them to the ranch hands. I know Blaze has a couple of guys coming out to help him since your dad isn't here anymore. You might have to give them some guidance. You were always out there helping him, even more so than Sam."

Sam.

The lump in my throat doubled in size at the mention of my brother. "Yeah, I'll help out if I need to. Just let me know."

"I'll tell Blaze."

"Great," I mumbled at the mention of his name again, adjusting the navy blue ballcap on my head. I was having a bad hair day to say the least, and a hat was the perfect solution. "I'll be back soon."

"Thank you for running errands for me, Beth." She gave me a smile and tiny wave, before turning her attention back to the corrals, where a couple of guys had appeared to watch the show as well.

"No problem." I headed down the steps toward my dad's old blue Ford. It felt wrong to drive his truck. It wasn't like I hadn't been through grief before. The moments of suffocation would fade to a dull throb. I knew it was better to drive the truck while it still smelled like his aftershave, than it was to get in it after the scent had faded to the stench of dirt and manure.

It didn't mean that it still didn't hurt, though.

I slid in and scooted the seat forward, fighting the urge not to climb right back out as the pain slammed into my chest.

It's just a truck, Beth. It's just a freaking truck.

Wiping my moist eyes, I fired it up and roared backward, spinning the tires and throwing gravel. I glanced in the rearview mirror, relieved no one noticed my overdramatic departure. Navigating the long gravel drive, I made it to the old highway. I made a left turn and headed toward town. The stretch of highway into Rustdale ran through mostly farm and ranch land, dotted with houses and cattle. It was a strikingly refreshing sight; better than the urban life I had lived —not that it changed how I felt about being there. I fidgeted with the radio, not surprised that it didn't work as static filled the truck. The thing had been broken longer than I had been alive.

The seven-mile drive went by in a blip. I pulled into the empty spot outside of the BNR Grocery store. My stomach instantly knotted up as I grabbed the list and my bag, already feeling anxious about seeing familiar faces. I glanced up in the rearview mirror, pulling my hat down a little further.

Maybe no one will recognize me.

Taking a deep breath, I opened the door and slid out. I pulled at the bottom of my old gray T-shirt, covering the waistband of my faded bootcut jeans. There was no doubt that I fit the bill of a small town woman in the moment. No one would probably guess that my normal attire for the last year had been pantsuits and heels.

Oof. I don't miss that.

I nearly laughed, heading into the grocery store. I grabbed a shopping cart and tossed my bag in, determined to make quick work of the tiny place. I could be in and out in twenty minutes.

I hope.

Mom had a lengthy list, and I found myself grumbling as I headed to the produce section. You'd have thought she was feeding a full house. I reached for a bag of potatoes when I heard my name—not even five minutes into the shopping trip.

"Oh my gosh! Beth Young? Is that you?"

Shit.

I spun around, immediately recognizing Sarah Armitage, an old friend—well, more like an acquaintance, but yeah. "Hi Sarah, it's been a long time." I gave her a smile as I carefully sat the potatoes into the cart.

"Oh, it has been forever!" she squealed so loud it nearly made me jump. "How have you been? I heard about your dad; I'm so sorry." She pulled me into an awkward, stiff hug that more than likely was only awkward because of me. "I was gonna come to the funeral, but I just had so much going on. You know how life can be—so busy. My niece, Lauren, competed for Rodeo Princess yesterday over in Gale, and I did her hair. You know I always did those Rodeo Queen pageants. But anyway, sorry about your dad." She rested her hand on my shoulder, batting her thick, fake eyelashes.

"Of course, thanks," I said with a nod. Sarah was the epitome of a small town princess. She was the Homecoming Queen, Prom Queen, Rodeo Queen—queen of anything that could be queened. "I really need to—"

"Girl, you look good." Sarah made a swooping motion, like a car salesman as she cut me off. "City life did you great, all of that walking to stay slim. I could use that kind of life. You still have that natural look about you though. I love it."

"Thanks, Sarah. But honestly, you look great yourself," I said. I meant it, too. I mean, sure, the tanning bed made her age a little faster, but overall, she looked as pretty as ever, her blonde hair spilling over her shoulders in waves. "I'm glad you're doing so well. Anyway, I should—"

"I am doing so good. How about you? Are you good? As good as you can be, I guess, considering your dad. Gosh, I'm just so sorry, I heard it was from a spider bite?" She tilted her head, her styled brows furrowed with sympathy.

Wow, does she ever just let someone finish talking? I thought. "Um... It was a wasp sting. He was allergic, but uh, I'm doing okay. I'm just in town helping my mom get everything settled. I probably won't be staying much longer than just—"

"Oh, you're not staying around?" she cut me off for third time, her hand landing lightly on my forearm, touching me again. "I figured since your mom was gonna be all alone now, it was just like a sign for you to move back home. My grandma Lin said that your mom's been prayin' for you to come back to town and stay."

I hesitated, the realization of my mom being truly alone hitting me. "Well, I'll be here to ensure that everything is settled and she's comfortable."

Sarah nodded, her smile shrinking a little. "That's nice of you to do that. I haven't talked with her in a long time, but I thought I might stop by and say hello sometime."

"Yeah, you should do that," I said, eyeing my grocery list—the one I hadn't even managed to mark a single item off of. "Mom always really liked you," I added, which was the truth. She did like Sarah. Everyone liked Sarah.

"Your mom is so sweet," she beamed, clasping her hands together. My eyes flickered to her left hand, noticing that it was missing a ring. *Huh. That's weird. I guess she and Lucas...*

"We got divorced about a year ago," Sarah answered my question, and I ripped my gaze away from her ring finger.

"I'm so sorry," I said, feeling more awkward than ever for staring. "I thought that, um, I just...wow, I'm so sorry."

She giggled, waving it off. "Oh, don't worry about it. I think the whole town has been talking about it well before Lucas and I ever split. It was hard to ruin that whole high-school-sweetheart kind of romance, but it happens. What about you? Last I heard, you were with that hot shot lawyer with the firm up in Chicago. But then you deleted your Facebook, and I don't see a ring on that finger, girl." She raised an eyebrow, motioning to my own bare ring finger.

"Our divorce was finalized a couple of months ago. Jared and I had been separated for quite some time though." I was careful not to spill much more than that, holding back about his twenty-four-year-old intern that was now his girlfriend. The last thing I needed was to give the town something to talk about. Sarah had always been the kind of woman that was friends with everyone.

And I still got that same vibe from her.

"Oh, wow, divorces are tough, but girl, I can already tell that you've got that post-breakup glow goin' on." Sarah waved her hand over me, motioning to a figure that I was certain had only gotten worse since the divorce.

But whatever. I'd take it.

"Thank you, Sarah. It's been really great talking with you," I said to her, holding up my list. "But Mom's waiting on me to get back with all the groceries. I don't want to keep her waiting too long."

"Oh, my goodness," she gasped. "I'm so sorry. I didn't mean to eat so much of your time up." Sarah smoothed out her black tank top, tucked carefully in the front of denim shorts. "It was just so nice catchin' up. We should meet for drinks tonight at Outlaws. They've got great deals for ladies on Monday nights."

Nothing like going to the bar on a Monday night.

"Uh...I don't know."

"Oh, come on, Beth," she pleaded, squeezing my arm. "You have to come out. We can meet there at eight, and I guarantee you'll be home before ten. I don't like to stay out late anymore."

I let out a heavy sigh, forcing a smile. "Okay. I'll meet you there around eight."

"Yay!" Sarah clapped her hands together like a little kid. "This is so great. I can't wait to catch up. It'll be perfect. It's gonna be the best night ever!"

CHAPTER THREE

I can do this.

My stomach lurched as I parked my dad's old truck outside of Outlaws, the small town honkytonk. I had never really gone to this bar, having left Rustdale long before I was of legal drinking age. That being said, I'd heard more than enough about it to know what I was getting myself into.

A lot of familiar faces.

I flipped the visor down, peering in the mirror at my lightly done makeup. I had never been one to really goop the stuff on, but I did like to accentuate my dark green eyes. I pushed a stray lock of auburn hair from my face and blew out a sharp breath.

"Just a couple of drinks and then I can go," I grumbled to myself as I slid out of the truck, opting for a flowy black halter tank and bootcut jeans. I looked cute, but I had tried not to look too cute. I didn't want to give off a single-and-ready-to-mingle vibe.

If that was even possible to do in Rustdale.

My phone buzzed in my pocket, and I pulled it out, seeing a text from my mom.

Have a good time!

Chuckling to myself, I texted her back a quick "Thanks!" feeling like I was a teenager all over again heading out for a night with my friends. It might've turned into a nostalgic moment, but my mind flashed back to my brother, Sam. I quickly pushed the thought of him away, not wanting to revisit the trauma wrapped up in those same feel-good years.

My boots crunched on the gravel as I headed toward the front door of the bar, noting a few men standing out front chit-chatting. I didn't recognize them, but they were clearly trying to recognize me as their eyes raked over my figure.

Gross.

"Hey, darlin'," one of them called as I pushed through the old saloon style door. I didn't even bother to acknowledge whoever said it, keeping my eyes focused straight ahead. The bar was smaller than I had imagined it would've been from outside, but there was still a decent-sized dance floor and a few tables. It didn't take but a second for my eyes to find a cute, overdressed blonde-haired woman at one of the central tables—smack dab in the middle of the room.

"Hey Sarah," I greeted her, forcing a smile as I climbed onto the tall chair. "This place is—"

"Authentic," Sarah finished for me. "I've always thought it looks just like the bars and honkytonks that you see on TV, like *Yellowstone* or something."

"I was gonna say it's a little loud," I laughed, shaking my head. "But yeah, I guess it's authentic, too."

She smiled. "I got you a beer. Well, actually, I got us a bucket of beers. It's so much cheaper that way. I hope you like Coors. I feel like everyone likes Coors."

"Yeah, of course, thanks," I said, taking one of the bottles from the bucket of ice. "I do like Coors, so this is perfect." I popped the top off, and took swig, trying not to people watch. However, I couldn't help myself. My eyes scanned the room, looking for any familiar faces. There were a few that seemed like maybe I *once* knew them—but I couldn't be sure.

"So, you said you're not staying here long?" Sarah's voice grabbed my attention. "Are you due back in, um..." Her eyes diverted to her phone sitting on the table beside her beer. She hit the lock button, looking up at me with a smile. "Chicago, right?"

"Yeah, that's where I worked at the firm with my ex-husband, but I actually quit. I don't really have anything planned right now. I figured I'd take the down time to figure out where I want to go from here."

"You know Greg is retiring soon." She perked up, leaning against her hand. "I know that 'cause Lucas was using him for some of his shit goin' on with the county."

"Oh?" I couldn't hide my surprise. "I never really pegged him as the type to get in trouble."

"Well, you know..." her voice trailed off as her gaze dropped to her hands, and then back up at me. "There's only so much to do in a small town. People get bored."

"Yeah, that's one way to put it," I chuckled, sipping on the beer. I had no intention of having more than just one, but that was solely because I didn't drink anymore. I had no idea what my limit was.

"Have you started dating again?" The question wasn't surprising, especially coming from Sarah. Mom had already made the subtle push toward Blaze—even in the middle of tragedy.

"I haven't," I answered her honestly. "I don't really think that I'm going to focus on that right now. I spent way too long caught up in a shitty relationship with someone who, at the end of the day, didn't care about me."

Her smile faded to a frown. "It sounds like you've really gone through some heartbreak. Lucas and I weren't really like that, I guess. We just... Well, he started getting involved in stuff that I wasn't okay with, so I finally set some boundaries." She let out a heavy, pained sigh. "And those boundaries led to divorce. Took the cops three weeks just to find him to serve him the papers."

I nodded, feeling sympathy for her. "Are you dating?" Normally, I wouldn't even ask a question like that, but I preferred the conversation to focus on her, rather than me. I was still just feeling... *numb.*

"Oh, you know," her demeanor quickly brightened. "I was always told the best way to move on was to find someone else."

Classy advice.

"And so, I take it that you've found a rebound then?" I gave her an amused look.

"More like rebounds," she beamed, giving me a sly look. "You'd be amazed at how much attention I got from all the men in this town after the divorce. It was just wild."

"I can only imagine." My tone was light and nonchalant, but in all truth, I felt a little hint of jealousy deep in my chest. When I got divorced, no one gave a shit about it.

"Yeah, girl, I have had *so* many suitors. Like, men have come out of the woodworks professing their undying love for me."

I laughed. "I'm not surprised. Everyone had a crush on you in high school."

"Oh my gosh, no," she played it off, but the way she flipped her blonde hair over her shoulder gave her away. "But let's see... Who would you know..." Sarah was in deep thought, her mouth in a flat line as her eyes shifted around the bar.

Take your time.

I pulled out my phone, glancing down to see a text from my mom. Before I could reply to it, however, Sarah spoke up.

"Oh, I've gone out a few times with Blaze Harris. He's the ranch manager over at your parents' place. He's super-hot and so charming, but he's totally emotionally unavailable."

"He's something," I managed to choke out, shifting uncomfortably in my chair. "I don't really know him though."

"Yeah, I'm waiting on his call, but he's busy like all the time." Sarah sounded annoyed just as her phone started vibrating against the tabletop. "Ugh, I swear..." Her eyes were on the phone again, but only for a split second. Sarah silenced it and flipped it over, screen down.

"You're popular," I teased, noticing that her smile had faded. "Just like always."

"Something like that. I've seen Ty Miller, Jack Carson, and um..." Sarah's hands went to her lap, and she leaned a little, looking right past me. "Garrett Myers has also been in the picture, too."

I froze at the name, feeling as though all the oxygen had been sucked right out of the room. "Oh?" was all I could manage as my stomach tightened, and I was suddenly reminded why I never came home.

"Yeah." Her eyes jumped from whatever was behind me to my face and then back to her phone, which I hadn't noticed buzzing again. "Anyway, I really need to use the restroom." Her voice shifted as she slid off the chair, grabbing up her phone. Something about the way she was acting was... off.

"Are you okay, Sarah?" I asked just as she turned to go.

"Oh yeah, for sure." She smiled at me, though it

didn't reach her pale blue eyes. "Um, just so you know, I already paid for the beer."

Before I could say anything, she spun on her heel and took off toward a hallway just off the dance floor.

What the hell was that about?

CHAPTER FOUR

Where is she?

I drummed my fingers on the table, noticing my smartwatch said it was nearly 10 p.m. Twenty minutes had passed since Sarah had left the table, and honestly, I was starting to worry. Maybe she was getting sick or something? Before I could second guess the decision, I slid off the chair and slung my bag over my shoulder. I already had a headache from the obnoxiously loud music and smoke, so a trip to the restroom didn't sound like such a bad idea.

The crowd was growing as it got later and that became more apparent as I weaved my way to the same hallway that Sarah had disappeared down. However, when I stepped into the dimly lit area I realized it wasn't the way to the restrooms at all.

What the hell?

The only thing in the hallway was a door at the end—that had a bright neon red exit sign overhead. I walked the length of the hallway just to double check I was right.

And yep, I was. Sarah Armitage had left me at the bar

to fend for myself.

No wonder she told me the beer was covered already.

I let out a heavy sigh, wondering if she was late for one of her many dates or if something else was bothering her. After all, she had seemed pretty nervous after her phone started blowing up. Regardless of her reasons, I was still here—and there was no way I was going to stay. I glanced back at the thickening crowd behind me and decided to take the same route Sarah had.

The warm breeze blew through my hair as I pushed through the exit, and even with the humidity, it was refreshing in comparison to the smoke-filled bar. I blinked my eyes a few times, adjusting to the darkness that surrounded me as the door clicked shut behind me.

***

Why are there no lights back here?

I didn't let myself ponder the question long, the crunching of something just off to the left sending a shiver down my spine. My head whipped in the direction, squinting into the blackness. The noise grew louder, and my entire body went rigid, ready to sprint away at any moment.

"Sarah?" I took a couple of stiff steps away from the noise, and suddenly the back lot was flooded with light from above me. However, I had no time to grumble about the faulty motion lights, the sight of a ghost standing right there in front of me.

"Beth?" He looked at me with pure disbelief. "I knew you'd probably be back in town, but I never thought you'd show up here."

"Yeah." I barely was able to choke out the response as I took in the sight of Garrett Myers. "I, um… I met a friend here for drinks. She left through this door, and I was just leaving to head home." I felt myself fighting the need to ramble, to fill the silence with meaningless words. However, I stopped myself, holding my tongue.

He studied me for a few moments, his chocolate eyes looking even darker in the night. "I haven't seen you in so long. You look all grown up." His voice was strained, thick with an emotion that triggered my heart to ache deep in my chest. "It was good to hear that you're back in town. I'm really sorry about your dad. He came to the shop sometimes—"

"Yeah, I don't come home much," I cut him off, the sound of his familiar voice making my stomach knot up so tight I thought I might double over. I tried not to look too hard at him, but I noticed that his face looked weathered beyond his thirty-six years. His shoulders were still broad and muscular, but they slumped from years of defeat. I knew he had turned to the bottle after my brother passed and, as much as I said I never held him responsible for what happened, it still hurt to see him.

"It's really good to see you." He took a step toward me, and my heart jumped as he stepped further into the light. There was a dark stain on his gray T-shirt, and I couldn't keep my eyes from drifting to it. "I work down at the mechanic shop these days," he said, having noticed me staring. "I should've gone home to change before coming out, but you know, everyone knows me. Everyone hates me, especially you, I'm sure." His voice was slightly slurred and paired with the redness in his eyes. "In case you were wondering, I'm just known as the drunk asshole to everyone now. That's what I grew up to be, while you're out making big bucks and screwing some high-class, fancy lawyer from New York City."

I bit my lip so hard a copper taste filled my mouth. "I don't hate you, Garrett. I never have, but I, um… I really need to get home." With that, I turned to go, heading in the opposite direction of him. However, I only took a couple of steps in before I felt a firm grip clamp down on my wrist. "What the hell?" I ripped my arm back from Garrett, my eyes wide. "What are you doing? I said I have to go home."

"I was just hoping that we could talk," he said quickly, his hands dropping to his sides. "I'd really like to talk, Beth. You're back in town, and I just want to—"

"Then talk to me when you're *sober*," I snapped, shaking my head as I stalked off. This time, he didn't follow me, and I was able to make it to the front parking lot without a hitch. There was a group of people outside smoking and talking, but I paid them no mind, my eyes focused only on the old blue Ford.

This was a terrible idea. The worst idea, actually.

I ripped at the handle of the truck, swinging it open and climbing inside. I slammed it shut and locked the doors before dropping my head into my hands. Of all the people to run into at the bar, Garrett was the last person I wanted to see. He was the epitome of everything I wanted to forget about this place—a reminder of the heartache and grief that swallowed the whole damn place.

"Ugh," I groaned as I started the ignition, wiping the tears from my cheeks. I hadn't even noticed that I had started to cry, and I hoped more than ever that it hadn't started in front of Garrett. He had been my brother's *best* friend growing up. He was once like family, sharing in a lot of the same memories as me.

And now I just wanted to run the moment I saw his face.

Sam wouldn't have wanted me to treat him that way.

The guilt slammed into my chest and the tears came more readily. The thought of my father, the kind man he was, visiting Garrett and keeping tabs on him. My dad had tried everything he could to keep the connection between Garrett and our family, but Garrett had pushed him out, running from the grace that Dad extended.

But I didn't help, not once.

As I looked up from my lap, I halfway expected to see Garrett in front of the truck, ready to bombard me all over again. But there was no one there, only the distant sound of laughter and country music. Shaking my head, I threw the truck into reverse and got the hell out of there, heading straight home.

I'll never do this again.

CHAPTER FIVE

"So did you have a nice time last night?" Mom asked me as I sat down in the rocking chair opposite her. "I didn't hear you come in."

I shrugged, taking a sip of the hot coffee—which did not pair well with a warm morning. "I'm surprised you didn't. I mean, I tried to be quiet, but the truck is loud enough to wake the whole county."

She pursed her lips, her eyes shifting out to the barn and corral, where Blaze and his hands were once again working with some of the ranch horses. "I took some sleeping pills." Mom's voice was quiet, and it was a little shocking, considering the woman never took anything—not even Tylenol for a headache.

"That's okay," I said, seeing the flash of guilt in her hazel eyes. "There's nothing wrong with that."

She nodded. "Just for now."

"Yeah, just for now." I glanced down at my cup of coffee, overloaded with creamer. I was struggling to find the words, knowing that she was hurting more than I was in the moment. My dad had been her whole world, and while she was stronger than most—and hardened from the loss of Sam—I knew that this wasn't easy for her.

I just wished that I knew how to be there for her.

"So, Sarah is good?" Mom spoke up, her tone brighter. "I haven't seen her in so long. Well, I take that back, actually. I see her around town all the time, but I never have a chance to actually talk with her. You know how that goes."

"Yeah, duck and run," I chuckled, relieved to see a smile tugging at her thin lips. "But yeah, she's good. Well, she says she is. She basically just left me at the bar in the middle of a conversation." I couldn't hide the confusion from my face.

Mom raised her brows at me. "That wasn't very thoughtful of her."

"Well, I don't know I would go that far with it," I said quickly. "She seemed to be a little… agitated, maybe? I don't know. Her phone just kept going off, and so maybe something was up."

"Huh," was all my mom said in response.

"Who knows. Drama probably."

"Maybe." She turned to me. "Did you see anyone else you know there? I figured that's where all the kids are at these days."

"Well, first of all, I'm almost thirty-four, so I don't know if that counts as being a kid. Secondly, um…" my voice trailed off as a lump caught in my throat, Garrett coming back to mind. "No, I didn't. I guess maybe I don't know everyone in town like I thought I did." I hated lying to her, but with dad's death still fresh, I hated the thought of drudging up the past even more.

"I always forget how fast the time goes by," Mom commented, getting a distant look in her eyes. "You blink and the years are gone. Although, I was expecting to have some grandchildren by now." She shot me a playful smirk to which I rolled my eyes, both of us laughing.

"Maybe someday when I actually find a man who's not a worthless piece of shi—"

"Language," Mom warned me but then made a face. "But yeah, Jared was a piece of shit. I'm glad that's over."

"Me, too, Mom. Me, too." I let out a sigh, my mind flashing back to the past nearly decade that I had wasted on Jared. There was a time that I had been severely broken up over it, but not anymore. The heartache was replaced by a potent reminder to not ignore all the red flags just because a man is handsome.

"You know, now that Dad is gone, I don't know who is going to keep up with Garrett. I'm sure you know that he was down there at that mechanic shop at least once a week."

I nearly spit the coffee right out of my mouth at the mention. "Oh?" I croaked, before clearing my throat. "I knew he visited him, but not that often."

"It's just heartbreaking. He's married now, you know."

"Wait, what?" I jerked back in my chair, shaking my head in disbelief. "Sarah mentioned that she was seeing him for a while."

Mom's brow furrowed. "Oh... But he's married to Brittany, she goes to our church sometimes. Maybe something happened though. I don't know. I don't keep up with the drama. I haven't seen any divorces in the paper though."

"It's not true if it hasn't made the paper," I mumbled under my breath, my eyes dropping to the coffee in my lap. There was a time that I thought I would always be here in Rustdale, starting a family of my own and letting the kids grow up on the ranch like I did. But that was ages ago.

"When do you think you'll go see Greg?" Mom's voice caught my attention. "I know that it's pretty cut and dry, but you know how those things are. I just feel like it's better to let the lawyers work through it."

I laughed. "I don't think Dad's will is very complicated, Mom. He probably just left everything to you."

"Well, no," Mom said, her lips pursed. "That's not what he did at all."

"What? What else would he have done?" My stomach knotted up. "There's no way that he would've put in a clause to sell the ranch or something."

"No, there's not a clause to sell, but I know that he gave you partial ownership...and honey, we aren't exactly doing well. There is a chance that we'll have to sell. We haven't been in the black for years. Savings floated us for most of the time, and then passed that... I don't know. We've had some big droughts. There's a lot you're gonna have to look over."

"So, what do you want to do, Mom?" I asked the question, my own emotions suddenly all over the place. I couldn't imagine the ranch not being a part of my family, but if the finances were really that bad. The land was worth a lot—millions, maybe.

"Oh, Beth," she waved me off. "It doesn't really matter what I want. I just want to set you up for a future that suits you. If that means sellin' the ranch, then so be it. I can move to town. Lord knows I can't keep up with all the management of this place. If it wasn't for Blaze, your father and I would've drowned three years ago. He works here for much less than he should. He also works part-time as a deputy for the county to make up for it."

So, Blaze is also a saint, too. Good to know.

I chewed the inside of my cheek, not even sure what to say to her. "I'll just have to go in and look at it, but just so you know," I paused, my heart squeezing with grief. "I'll figure out a way to keep you here on this ranch if possible. As hard as it is for me to be in this town, there's no way I can handle moving you off to some townhouse, just so I can put some cash in our pockets."

She gave me a grateful smile, however, it quickly faded as the sound of sirens filled the air. "What in the world?"

I whipped my head toward the ever-growing noise, which was quickly accompanied by the sound of tires on the gravel drive. My head jerked back toward the corrals, where the guys had ceased their training session, all eyes looking past the back porch to the front yard—which was out of our line of sight.

My heart began to beat in my throat as a County Sheriff's truck came roaring around the back of the house, stopping to park in the gravel, not far from the blue truck I had driven home. Mom and I watched in silence as Sheriff Myers stepped out of the vehicle. He had a grim look on his face as he adjusted his Stetson cowboy hat before heading in our direction.

"Do you know what this is about?" I turned to Mom, giving her a curious look.

"No..." Mom's voice trailed off as she glanced over at me, and then out to where Blaze was opening the corral gate. "If anything, Sheriff Myers only ever comes by if it's to talk with Blaze."

The sheriff gave us a nod as he approached the old back porch, climbing the steps in a way that was almost painful. "Good morning, ladies."

"Sheriff Myers," Mom said to him, her voice cautious. "What can we do for you?"

"Well," he began, his gray eyes surrounded by matching dark circles on his weathered skin. "I was wondering if I could have a word with your daughter."

"Me?" I asked stupidly, pointing to my chest.

"Yep, you."

CHAPTER SIX

I followed Sheriff Myers back toward his truck, pausing to look back at my mom, whose eyes were nearly as wide as her oval face. "Um, would you mind telling me what this is about?" I shifted my attention back to the sheriff, whose slim frame walked with a slight forward lean.

He stopped when we made it to his truck. Turning around, he leaned his body against the hood. "Well, for starters, why don't you tell me where you were last night."

There was something in his voice that rang my lawyer alarm bell. "I went out for some drinks with Sarah Armitage and then I came home." My gaze flickered over to Blaze, who had joined my mom on the porch, his eyes trained in my direction. "Is something wrong, Sheriff Myers?"

He let out a heavy sigh before removing his cowboy hat and setting it on the hood. "Yeah, actually something is wrong, Miss Young. What time did you leave the bar last night?"

My stomach began to churn at the routine questions.

"Um, somewhere around ten, I think. It might've actually been a little before."

"And can anyone confirm your arrival time home?"

I bit my lip. "I...I mean, yeah, probably. I don't really get where you're going with this though," I added quickly, my voice shifting from nervous to stern. He had caught me off-guard, but I wasn't going to stay that way.

"Sarah Armitage's body was found this morning under Hollow Creek Bridge, just a mile and a half from here. Now, according to some of the fellas in town, they said they saw you with her at Outlaws last night."

I blinked at him a few times, still trying to process what he was saying. "Wait, Sarah is... dead?"

His eyes bore into mine, mirroring that of his son's—though not reddened by alcohol. "That is what I just said, Beth. Now, I just need you to tell me anything and everything that you can remember about last night, and don't leave anything out."

I swallowed hard, replaying the events. "Um, yeah, of course. I met Sarah for drinks around eight-thirty. I was running late. We chatted for about an hour. I don't know." I shook my head. "I just know that her phone was going off like crazy and she kept silencing it." Sheriff Myers nodded, jotting things down on a notepad. "After that, it was probably like nine-thirty when she randomly said that she needed to go to the restroom. She never came back."

That last bit caught his attention and his head jerked

upwards. "So what? She just left?"

"Um, well, I watched her walk down the far hallway at the back of Outlaws. I didn't realize that was not where the restrooms were. When she hadn't returned for like twenty minutes, I went looking for her and saw the only thing at the end of the hallway was an exit to the back." I could feel myself beginning to ramble, but I kept myself in check. I was a lawyer for heaven's sake. I knew how to handle the police.

Though I've never been the one being questioned about a crime.

"Okay, so what did you do when you couldn't find her? And did you by chance see who she had been talking to on her phone?" His tone had lightened a little, probably because I was obviously cooperating with him to the best of my ability.

"I don't know who she was talking to," I admitted. "I only know that her phone just kept going off, over and over. She seemed more annoyed by it than anything else. But anyway," I shook my head, some of my messy hair falling from my bun on top of my head. "I, uh, I went out the back door—"

"To look for Sarah?" he interjected.

Putting words in my mouth.

"No, actually," I corrected him. "I honestly just assumed that she had gone somewhere else. She's a grown woman, and I don't really know her that well."

"So then why were you out for drinks with her?"

"Uh, because we ran into each other at the grocery store, and she asked me." I felt confused as I explained —and also... *guilty.* Why didn't I look harder for her? I should've called her or something. "I hadn't seen her since high school, to be honest."

"Yeah, okay, so you accept the random invitation to go out for drinks, then what?" Sheriff Myers was a hard man to read, his tone continuing to change sentence by sentence. First, he's pissy, then he's bright and friendly, and now he was just monotone.

"I stepped outside the back of the bar, thinking that it would keep me from having to go back through the crowd. It was starting to get super busy."

"And did you see anything suspicious?"

I hesitated, that eerie somber feeling creeping over me. "No, not really."

"Not really?"

"I saw..." my voice trailed off as I squeezed my eyes shut and took a deep breath.

Why was it so hard to say his name?

"Who did you see, Beth?"

"Garrett."

Sheriff Myers' mouth twitched, though his expression remained the same. "Like my son, Garrett? Or a different Garrett?"

"Your son," I said quietly. "I stepped out the back door and the motion lights didn't come on immediately. I don't know why. I don't know what he was doing back there."

"Stumbling around drunk, probably," he grunted in a barely audible voice. "Anyway, tell me what happened next."

"Uh, we had a very short conversation and then I left."

"What did you talk about with him?" Sheriff Myers asked but then stopped himself, letting out a quick audible breath. "It doesn't matter, actually. Um..." he shook his head. "Did you see anyone else on your way out?"

"No. Wait," I corrected myself. "There was a group of people standing right out front, but I didn't know who they were. I don't think they even noticed me leaving. I went straight home after that and went to bed."

And barely slept.

"Okay, and you didn't see any signs of Sarah once you exited the bar?" His eyes locked with mine, and I could see something there that wasn't when we had first started our conversation. "Anything that stands out? It might not mean anything to you, but it could mean a break in the case for us."

I nodded in understanding. "I can't think of anything."

Except for the spot on his shirt.

My mind replayed the massive dark stain on Garrett's gray T-shirt and my stomach lurched. It had been too dark to see what color it was.

"Beth?" Sheriff Myers caught my attention. "Did you see something?"

I chewed the inside of my cheek, the dark stain still at the forefront of my mind. "No. I don't think so. I was just so tired and ready to get home."

He nodded slowly. "Well, if you think of anything, you make sure and tell me. You know where to find me, and if you don't want to take a trip down to the office, just give the main number a call. There's always someone there answering the phones."

"Right." I could feel the eyes of my mother and Blaze still on my back as Sheriff Myers headed back around to the driver's side door of his pickup. "Sheriff?"

He jerked his head back in my direction. "Yeah?"

"I hope you find who did this."

"Yeah, me, too. Don't leave town or anything." With that, he slammed the door shut and started the engine. He backed out fairly quickly and was halfway down the driveway before I even turned around to head back to the porch. My stomach felt sick, and my heart was pounding unevenly in my chest.

I just saw her.

My head started to spin as I climbed the porch steps, my mom and Blaze still quiet. "Sarah was... She was murdered last night." I looked at my mom, her straight lips instantly turning to a frown.

"Murdered?"

"That's what I'm assuming," I said quickly. "Sheriff said they found her body under Hollow Creek Bridge. I don't know why else he would be questioning me the way he was."

"Did you know?" Mom turned to Blaze, who was standing solemnly on the porch, his eyes on his dusty boots.

"I, uh, yeah. I wasn't on duty, but Sean called me last night." He looked up, his eyes drifting to mine. "But I had no idea that you were out with her, Beth."

I felt a lump growing in my throat, the guilt returning. "I think I might've been the last person to see her, actually."

Mom's mouth dropped open as she gasped. "Oh no." Her hand flew up to cover it.

"Ah shit," Blaze muttered, his eyes diverting from mine and back out toward the barn. "I guess it's a good thing you're a lawyer then."

I narrowed my eyes at him as his gaze made it back to me. "Very insensitive joke there, Blaze."

"If we don't laugh, we might cry," he responded, giving me a shrug as he headed down the porch steps and back out toward the corral.

I turned to my mom. "I don't think I like him."

Mom shook her head. "He's just hardened like the rest of us. Let's head in. I bet this will make the news."

Yeah, probably so.

CHAPTER SEVEN

The evening came with no information—or news stories. Part of me was relieved, and the other part was battling the guilt of not looking for her a little harder.

Or just freaking following her to the restroom.

I squeezed my eyes shut for a moment as I tried to take a deep breath, the humidity feeling more suffocating than ever as I stopped just outside of the barn. Mom had spent the entire day avoiding calls from church friends and watching her social media page like a hawk, waiting for the news to break in the town. But it hadn't yet.

I slid the barn door open, having been asked to feed the horses their evening meal. My body felt heavy as I trudged across the old concrete floor. It had been really nice back in the day, built nearly fifty years ago. But now, even though it had been kept up to the best of my parents' ability, it wasn't the grandiose place that was often shown on TV. It had an ever-lingering smell of dirt and manure no matter how often it was cleaned, and the concrete was chipping from years of wear and tear.

Shaking my head, I grabbed the buckets and headed into the small feed room. My eyes landed on the dry erase board, taking in the sight of my dad's handwriting. It hit a chord deep in my chest, but I pushed it away. The best way for me to deal with grief was to just keep going. Don't get me wrong, there was a time to cry. But it wasn't right then, especially with Sarah's murder hanging over my head.

"Everything is going to be fine," I said to myself under my breath as I scooped out some of the feed, tossing it into the closest bucket. I wasn't sure if I believed my own words, but someone had to say it.

"So, saying affirmations in the barn is your thing?" A deep chuckle erupted from behind me.

I let out a heavy sigh, turning around to see Blaze—this time in his cute little deputy uniform. "Ah, so this is why Mom said I have to do the evening feed shift."

"That would be why," he replied, shaking his head at me.

I hated the way his cowboy hat accentuated his square jaw, shadowed with just enough stubble to be considered by some as sexy. "Good to know," I choked out, spinning back around to focus on filling the buckets. While it was tempting to use the cowboy turned law enforcement as a much-needed distraction, I knew what it would lead to. *Heartbreak.*

"So, Beth…"

My shoulder slouched as I realized he hadn't taken

the cue to leave. "Yeah?" I said from where I was hunched over the large bin, digging the quart scoop into the pellets.

"Not to be nosy, but..."

But he's going to be nosy.

"What were you doing out with Sarah? Your dad always said that you never associated with anyone from town."

I dumped another scoop of grain and looked up at him, blowing a puff of air to move my hair from my eyes. "Uh, honestly, she cornered me at the store, and I don't know," I threw my hands up in frustration. "I accepted the offer for drinks because God knows I needed one after the shitty week I've had. Why?"

He raised one of his dark eyebrows at me. "I was just curious."

"I got a question for you then," I shot back at him, folding my arms across my chest.

Blaze chuckled, shrugging his shoulders. "Okay. What's your question?"

"Where were *you* last night?"

His easy smile quickly faded. "Really?"

"I mean, according to Sarah," I began, tugging my damp T-shirt free from my sweaty abdomen. "The two of you were kind of seeing each other."

I swear the light went right out of his hazel eyes, though he played it off coolly. "She told you that, huh?

Did you ask her about me?"

"Ha," I rolled my eyes. "Like I would ask her about you. No, actually, she offered it up and said that she was waiting on you to call her back or something."

He nodded. "Well, if it puts that pretty little mind of yours at ease, I wasn't really interested in Sarah. If you knew her to any extent, you know that she kind of had this way of fenagling into your life—if that's what she wanted to do."

The past tense talk of her caught me off guard. "Yeah, I guess I get that."

"So, no, I had no intention of calling her. We went on two dates, both of which were just drinks there at Outlaws after I got off my shift. Never even left the bar with her."

"Right," I said, embarrassment creeping into my cheeks as I realized how stupid I was for picking at something I had no clue about. "Got it. Thanks for the clarification."

"Yeah, anytime. Would you like to know about my other past dates?" He gave me an amused grin that made my heart flip, but I ignored it. I knew better than to listen to that old thing.

"I have no interest in knowing anything more about your dating life," I grumbled, turning back to the feed bin—and that was true mostly.

"If you say so," he said from behind me. I could feel his presence still there, lingering in the doorway. "But

Beth?"

Ugh. Why will he not just go away?

I exhaled sharply, dumping more feed into a third red bucket. "Yes, *Blaze*?"

"I was here last night, sitting on my ass watching TV after a long day," he said, his eyes locking with mine as I glanced back up to him. "That was the original question you asked, you know. Seeing that you're a lawyer, I wouldn't have expected you to let that one go unanswered. It's much more relevant to the case, hon." There was a teasing tone to his voice, as a smile tugged his lips upward.

I narrowed my eyes at him. "Mmm, thank you for filling in the gap."

"Anytime." He shot me a wink.

I wanted to slap the smirk right off his face as he finally turned to go, leaving my head even more of a wreck than before. Grumbling to myself, I finished filling the buckets and then arranged them in the cart. I made my way down the aisle, dumping them into each stall per the label overhead.

As I reached the final stall, my heart squeezed as I looked in. *Jhett.*

My father's old black gelding greeted me with a nicker, poking his head out of the stall. He had been the last of the horses my dad had personally trained and that was years ago, making Jhett nearly twenty-four years old. He looked to be in good shape as I stroked his forehead and filled his trough with grain.

"I know you miss Dad," I choked out, my emotions catching up to me as Jhett hungrily dug into the feed—like he wasn't fed copious amounts of the highest quality stuff with a workload of zero. I watched him for a few moments longer before leaving him to finish in peace. I put the cart and buckets away, before stopping to take a seat on one of the stools in the feed room.

I pulled my phone from my pocket and went to Google, unable to help myself. I typed in Sarah Armitage, and then hit the search button. I held my breath as I waited for the page to load, halfway expecting to see the news of her death plastered all over the results.

But there was nothing.

"What the hell?" I muttered, shaking my head at the screen. Since when did someone—someone who happened to be a bright young woman—get murdered and it not show up everywhere. Even in Chicago, the murder capital of the USA, there would've been some sort of report hitting the news by now.

I stared at the screen a little longer, before locking it and putting it back in my jeans pocket. I knew how criminal investigations went all too well. And it had been my job to defend the guilty—well, sometimes not guilty, but mostly, I defended the bad guys. I had never wanted to be a criminal defense attorney, but it had been thrown in my lap, and honestly, I was good at it.

But that life felt like a distant memory in the

moment.

CHAPTER EIGHT

"Listen, I'm just going to cut to the chase," Greg, our family attorney said. "The financials are in bad shape, Beth. I think your best bet is to sell. He left you in charge of making the decisions when it comes to the place, because he knew you could make the hard decisions."

I stared at him, blinking a few times. "They're not that bad." I glanced back down at the papers sitting in front of me. The moment I started going over them, I knew exactly why my mom had put me up to the task. Sifting through the debts and underpayments was grueling.

"Sure, if you have two-hundred-fifty thousand dollars laying around," Greg said with a sigh. "And that's just barely scratching the surface."

"Why did they take out a line of credit?" I groaned, facepalming myself. "I don't know why they didn't just sell off some of the equipment to pay for these."

"Well, your father was a stubborn man, and you and I both know that he was not going to give in to anyone else's advice. He's defaulted a hundred times over."

"So, you'd been telling him to sell off some assets

to pay this shit off, right?" I leaned my elbow against the conference room table, resting the side of my head against my hand.

"I've been working on him for years to get this sorted, thinking of the mess that it would leave behind if he didn't get it ironed out. He didn't listen, and now you and Andrea are having to suffer the consequences."

"Did Mom not know?" I studied his face, watching lines gathering around his eyes as he hesitated. He had to be at least ten years my mom's senior—and I was pretty sure that we were related somewhere down the line.

"She kind of knew, but she put all her trust in your dad." He paused, letting out a heavy sigh. "I really don't know what else to tell you, Beth. You got stuck with a hard decision. Honestly, my advice would be to sell the ranch, cut your losses, and use the money to buy your mom a house in town. You'll make plenty to put away for your kids someday."

"I want my future kids to be able to see where I grew up," I countered.

"Well, you can point it out to them when you drive past."

I narrowed my eyes at him, biting my tongue from a response out of anger. "I don't think I can sell the ranch. It would absolutely devastate Mom, even if she's not showing it right now. I have nearly one-hundred-fifty thousand in savings. Will that keep the debt collectors at bay?"

Greg's face dropped. "Don't lose your life savings on the ranch."

"I can build it back up," I said with a shrug. "It's just money." I hesitated as the emotions began to swell in my chest. "Greg, she's all I have left. I don't want to dump her off in some house in town."

He nodded. "That's up to you. Take those." Greg gestured to the papers. "Once you've had a chance to really look them over and think about it, you come back and see me."

I gathered up the sheets, shoving them into my messenger bag. I had dressed a little nicer for the visit, putting on a pair of dark wash trousers and a white blouse. I slung my black bag over my shoulder and rose to my feet.

"Thanks," I forced a half-hearted smile. "I'll try and come up with something over the next few days."

"Yeah, of course, Beth." I turned to go, trying not to feel like I was drowning.

"Oh, one more thing," Greg's voice caught me as I opened the door.

"What's that?" I stopped to look back at him.

"I have some good connections in the DFW area. It'd be a great way for you to be close without being too close, if you know what I mean."

"I'll keep that in mind," I said, giving him a grateful half-smile. "Right now though, I'm just trying to take it day by day. I won't be leaving town any time soon."

Mostly because Sheriff Myers said so.

"Good for you to put your mom first like that," Greg's gaze was full of sympathy. "Y'all sure haven't had it easy. But did you hear about Sarah Armitage?" he added suddenly. "I saw it on the news first thing this morning. I just can't even believe it."

My mouth went dry at the mention. "Yeah, it's really horrible."

"Shot to death." He shook his head, despair written all over his face. "Can't even fathom who the hell would wanna hurt that woman. Everyone loved her."

I nodded. "It's unbelievable in the worst kind of way." With that, I slipped out of the conference room, quickly making my exit from the law office. I hadn't checked the news since the night before, and obviously, I had missed them finally breaking the story.

The air was muggy as I stepped outside, but dark gray clouds were covering the sun. It at least gave the illusion that it was cooler than it had been. My eyes drifted to the old truck waiting for me, parked right off the street. I headed toward it, already dreading the conversation I was bound to have with Mom when I made it home. But as much as it made sense to sell the ranch, it just wasn't going to happen. She wouldn't have to worry about that.

I stepped down off the sidewalk and reached for the handle. "Beth!" a deep voice caught my attention. "Beth, is that you?"

Shit.

I plastered a smile on my face as I looked up, expecting to see someone who went to church with my parents or something, but instead, the face I saw made my chest feel tight. "Hey, Lucas."

"Hey," he sounded out of breath with his snapback hat on backwards and his rugged complexion dotted with beads of sweat. "I was hoping to catch you around."

"Yeah?" I studied his faded, stained jeans with a wrinkled red T-shirt. "What can I do for you?"

"Uh, see, I was talking to Ty and Gabriel, and they said they saw you at Outlaws with Sarah the night she… you know." His face contorted with emotion, and for a moment, I thought he might break down in tears right there on the sidewalk.

"I was there with her," I admitted, my eyes searching around the empty street as I tried to remember what those two guys even looked like. "But not very long. She left before I did."

He nodded; his expression was difficult to read. He had once been one of the most popular guys in school—the cliché quarterback of the football team and what not—and had been with Sarah since sophomore year. "I just wanna know if you saw anything."

"I didn't see anything but her walk toward the exit." I chose my words carefully. I didn't even actually see her leave the place. I just made that assumption. "I'm so sorry that you're going through this."

"You just lost your dad, right?" he countered, his voice going up a notch.

I tugged on the handle, opening the door a little. "Yeah, I did."

"How'd you lose him, if you don't mind me asking."

Well, I do. But whatever.

"He was allergic to wasps and was stung."

"Damn, that's brutal." Lucas said, though his voice seemed devoid of any real sympathy. "So, what did Sarah tell you that night?"

"Um, I don't know what you mean. We just had a couple of drinks and then she left. That's it," I reiterated.

"Right, but did she mention me? Did she mention the divorce?"

I couldn't tell if he was searching for some kind of closure or if he was angry with me, his tone of voice growing more strained by the second. "Lucas, she briefly mentioned the divorce when I ran into her at the grocery store, but we didn't get far into the conversation. We were just talking, and she said she had to go..."

"Go where?"

Jeez.

"She said to the restroom, but she never came back," I said quickly before throwing up a hand as if I was swearing on a Bible. "I don't know anything more than that."

"Was Garrett there?"

I knew the color drained right out of my face by the shifting expression on Lucas's.

"He was there, wasn't he? He's always there!" Without warning, Lucas's fist slammed down onto the hood of my truck, rage turning his face red. "He had something to do with it. I know he did!"

I took a step to the side, situating my body just behind the truck door. It put something between us, just in case. "I'm really sorry for what happened. I know that it can't be easy—"

"And you know what?" Lucas cut me off, his voice still oozing with anger. "His daddy down there at the sheriff's office ain't gonna do a thing about Sarah. He's just too busy tryin' to cover up his son's messed up head!"

My chest tightened a little more as I slid a little further behind the door. "I don't know. I just really need to get home."

"He's a loser, Beth. He did somethin' to her," Lucas continued to rant. "Just like he killed your brother!"

"I have to go," I nearly shouted, making a lunge for my truck's driver's seat. I slammed the door and locked it in one big swoop, barely able to breathe as I fumbled for the keys.

"You gotta help me do something about it!" Lucas continued to yell, jerking on the door handle.

My hands shook as I finally located the keys at the

bottom of my bag, and I shoved them into the ignition. The truck roared to life. I shot backwards into the street, leaving Lucas standing in the empty parking spot.

He threw his hands into the air at me, still just as infuriated as before. "What the hell, Beth!" But I could hardly hear him as I zoomed off down the street.

CHAPTER NINE

"A woman was found shot to death beneath a rural bridge just off County Road 880. The body has been identified as thirty-three-year-old Sarah Armitage of Rustdale, Texas. Blaine County Sheriff's Office is not releasing any other information as the investigation is ongoing. If you have any information on what happened to Sarah, please call the department. We've listed their contact information on the screen."

I stared at the television; Sarah's face plastered across the screen for a few seconds longer. The news then switched to an aerial shot of the crime scene after the fact, showing the old wooden bridge, the only crossing point over Hollow Creek. Nausea rolled over me as the camera zoomed down to the creek bed full of unmoving, stagnant water. The cameraman's voice signified that this was where she had been found. I shuddered at the thought of her body being left there—the audacity to just leave her there like she wasn't a human being.

"It's just horrible," Mom said, her voice quiet. "They're having the funeral service tomorrow at the church for her... I offered to make a casserole."

I nodded, though I fought the urge to combat my mother's need to supply food, like she still wasn't in need of help herself. I decided to avoid it. "It feels so surreal that I literally just saw her," I remarked. However, the sound of the side door opening caught my attention, and I looked over to my mom in her recliner. "Who is that?"

Mom's eyes never left the television, her voice flat. "Just Blaze. He's the only other one that has a key to the house."

"Right," I muttered, just as he stepped into the meager ranch-style living room.

"Hey, Mrs. Young," he greeted my mom with a tip of his hat before turning to me. "Beth, I need to speak with you."

I raised my eyebrows, unamused. "Why?" I struggled not to admire his athletic figure in his deputy uniform, so I diverted my gaze back to the news. I could feel Blaze's eyes boring into the back of my head.

"Uh, well, apparently there was an incident outside of Greg Mort's law office today."

My heart jumped. *Shit.*

"What in the world happened?" My mom gasped, her eyes going wide as they bounced between Blaze and me. "Beth, did you see anything?"

"The details are a little fuzzy," Blaze replied, his tone sharp. "But according to Lucas Armitage, Beth thought it might be a good idea to nearly run him over."

"That is not what happened!" I jumped to my feet as horror filled my mom's face. "He was shouting at me. He hit the hood of the truck. I think he put a dent in it. He was going batshit crazy on me!"

Blaze's facial expression changed. "He was going what?"

Ugh! I let out a heavy sigh as I tried to get ahold of my emotions. I wasn't usually the type to lose my cool, but jeez, the things this town brought out in me. "I was heading back to the truck from Greg's office when Lucas came out of nowhere. He started interrogating me and then he started talking about seeing Garrett that night. Then he mentioned... he mentioned Sam." Blaze and Mom were both quiet for a few moments. "But FYI, I didn't even come close to hitting him with the truck."

I don't think, anyway.

"You saw Garrett that night?" Blaze questioned; his brows furrowed. "That's not anywhere in the report."

"What? Why wouldn't it be in the report? I told Sheriff Myers when he was here that I saw Garrett when I left out the back of Outlaws. I talked with Garrett for a few minutes and then I left the bar, coming straight home."

"You saw Garrett? Why didn't you tell me?" Mom's question felt out of place, and all I could do was shrug in the moment at her.

"I don't know, Mom. I haven't talked to him in years, and he was so drunk. At least I think he was. His eyes were bright red, and his words were slurring. I know he's basically the town alcoholic now, and I don't—"

"Beth," I felt a warm hand on my shoulder. "Take a deep breath."

I looked up at Blaze, catching a whiff of his masculine cologne before I shrunk away. "I don't even know you. Don't touch me."

"Elizabeth Marianne Young," Mom snapped. "That was completely uncalled for."

I shook my head, all of the emotions making my body feel hot. "I can't do this right now." And before either of them could say anything else, I stormed through the living room and kitchen, ripping the back door open. It was still light out as I stepped onto the porch, trying to take a full breath.

Freaking Garrett. Of all the people.

Squeezing my eyes shut, I tried to think about anything else, but the trauma came flooding back in the sound of the crash, the sirens, the distinct smell of burning oil, my brother's cries, and the blood—*oh my gosh,* the blood. My stomach lurched violently, and I doubled over, barely making it to the edge of the porch before I lost my dinner.

"Oh, Beth." Mom's hand landed on the small of my back as I was still leaning over.

I wiped my mouth and stood up straight, backing away from her touch. "I'm sorry. I just... I don't know. Every time I come home, all I can think about is Sam."

She nodded, tears welling up in her eyes. "It's been over sixteen years, and if I let my mind go, I feel like it was just yesterday. I know how difficult it was for you—you were there. But Beth, you have to hold onto the good memories of him. Let the bad ones go."

"Mom, I watched my brother die because his dumbass friend was driving like an idiot. I don't like this town...I don't like being here. It's torture." Saying the words out loud made me sound so hateful, but it was the truth.

My mom nodded, giving me an understanding look. "You don't have to stay here, Beth. I know what you experienced was devastating. Maybe we should schedule an appointment with Pastor Frank. He helped me and your dad so much after Sam passed."

"I've gone through therapy and it's still always there in the back of my mind, threatening to come up in a bad dream or an off day. I miss him, and maybe you and dad got through it because you didn't have to see it. You weren't there." It felt terrible to throw that at her, like somehow, she hadn't experienced what I had. I knew it wasn't true, but my mouth was moving faster than my brain.

"You shouldn't have been there," Mom said, her voice strained. "I was supposed to pick you up that night from Sarah's graduation party, not Sam. It's just as much my fault that everything happened. Just like it's my fault that your dad didn't have his EpiPen that day he was out brush hogging. I took it out of the toolbox months ago."

"Mom, no. None of it your fault. Not dad and not Sam," I corrected her, adamantly shaking my head. "It's not your fault. It's…" my voice trailed off, thinking of Garrett. "I don't know whose fault it is."

She pursed her lips at me, as if I was still missing the point. "We don't live in a perfect world, Beth. People die for reasons that don't seem fair, and there are consequences for our actions. But you know, there're also plenty of times that people do stupid things, and nothing happens. Sometimes it's just luck of the draw. God just takes people home sometimes."

"I guess so," I mumbled, the taste of vomit still in my mouth. "But anyway, I just don't know why Lucas came at me like that about Garrett. He acted like Garrett had… killed her."

She chewed her bottom lip as she plopped down in the rocking chair, a somber expression on her face. "I don't know much about Garrett's life these days. Your dad never really told me much anyway, to be honest. He visited him often down at the auto shop, but he kept the conversations confidential. For Garrett's sake, I think."

I nodded, hesitating as a burning question came to my mind. "Mom…"

"Yeah?" She looked more tired than ever, dark circles under her eyes as she rocked slowly, her black sweatpants and bleach-stained T-shirt a couple of sizes too big. "What is it, Beth?"

"Do you think he did it?"

"What?" She tilted her head in confusion.

"Do you think Garrett could've killed Sarah?" The question left my lips just as Blaze stepped out onto the back porch, his eyes widening.

Mom paused, before blowing out a sharp breath. "I don't know. I don't know Garrett very well anymore. That would be a great question for your dad."

I nodded, a lump growing in my throat. *If only he were here.*

"Maybe I should talk to Garrett," I said, my stomach knotting up at the thought.

"That's a terrible idea," Blaze cut in, his voice stern. "You might be a lawyer, but you'll just impede the investigation or put yourself in danger."

I rolled my eyes at him, the dried tears on my cheeks feeling sticky—I was tired of feeling defeated. "Blaze, I know not to impede an investigation. I do this stuff for a living."

"Do you? Because rumor has it that you've started a new career as a stunt driver."

There was a moment of silence between all three of us standing there on the porch, and then I burst into laughter, Mom and Blaze joining me. After all, if I didn't laugh, I might just keep crying.

And I had already made my mind up. No more crying for me. I wanted answers.

CHAPTER TEN

"Holy crap, it's packed in here," I grumbled to Mom as we stepped into the church.

"Beth, we are in church," she warned me, shooting me a glare. "That language is so disrespectful. Can you please tone it down a notch?"

"Don't all lawyers go to hell anyway?" I stifled a giggle as she rolled her eyes at me. "Sorry, Mom," I added, giving her a half-hearted smile.

We slid into one of the back rows of the sanctuary, which probably was easily over its maximum capacity. There were a lot of familiar faces, but also a lot of unfamiliar ones. I swallowed hard, noticing a few people glance back at me—one of those faces being Lucas.

Ugh.

I diverted my eyes to Blaze, who was standing in the front corner of the old sanctuary in his uniform, his arms folded across his chest. There were law enforcement officers from multiple agencies scattered about, but their presence wasn't surprising—I knew the drill. Though the U.S. Marshal in the back did cause me a little confusion.

Why would a Marshal be involved? There must be a lot of movement in the case.

The U.S. Marshal looked on high alert, though not unrelaxed. It was easy to see that he was one of those seasoned kind of guys, with a permanently fatigued face and dulled eyes. Handsome to some degree though, with his broad shoulders and chiseled jaw. As if he could sense my gaze fixed on him, he turned his head in my direction, locking eyes.

Oops.

I quickly looked away, scanning the room. There was one face that I had yet to see in the sea of faces, and while I never thought I'd be doing it, I wanted to talk to Garrett. Rolling my shoulders to relieve some of the tension, I shifted in the pew beside my mom.

Mom leaned over, whispering. "You okay?"

I nodded, dropping my eyes to the bright, smiling face of Sarah Armitage on the funeral program sitting in my lap. The photo appeared recent, though it was hard to be certain. Her blue eyes were potent, as if they were boring into mine from the page. Crushing guilt rushed back, making my chest suddenly feel tight. I flipped the paper over abruptly, shaking my head as the piano began to play.

Mom's hand landed on mine, giving it a light squeeze. I looked over at her just in time for her to give me a reassuring half-smile. I returned it before focusing on finding Garrett.

Why is he not here? Where would he be?

My mind ran back to the lingering question I had after talking with Blaze in the living room. Why wasn't it in the report that I had spoken with Garrett that night? I mean, yeah, I understood that more than likely Garrett had no clue as to what was going on, too drunk to process anything. But I just couldn't let go of that stain—the one that I didn't mention in the interview. *Why did I hold that back? Did I hold back anything else?*

I could hardly hear the alto singing *I'll Fly Away*, her voice sounding distant as my ears began to ring. My knee bounced nervously, and I blinked to clear my blurry vision. It was as if I were on the verge of passing out, except I wasn't.

"She was her daddy's sweetheart, her momma's angel, and to know her was to love her," Pastor Frank began, his voice solemn. "What happened was horrific and has left us all reeling." Everyone nodded, a few muffled sobs breaking out across the room. I glanced over to my mom, whose eyes were glassy with moisture as well.

Everyone loved her. Well, someone didn't... Or maybe they loved her too much.

My thoughts were bugging me as I continued to try and pay attention to one of Sarah's brothers reading her obituary, adding his own commentary. However, he wasn't quite finished when the doors of the church were slung open, the sound of the handle slamming into the wall echoing through the sanctuary. I spun around, my mouth dropping open.

Oh no. No, no, no.

My eyes locked with Garrett's as he stumbled into the church, his eyes red and clothes ruffled. It appeared he had attempted to make himself look nice, his jeans starched and western button down mostly clean. But then it's like he rolled around on the floor—a lot.

"Get him out of here!" a voice called out as the music abruptly stopped.

"Shut the hell up, Ty," Garrett bellowed, pointing him out of the crowd. He then turned his attention right back to me. "Beth, we need to talk. It ain't cool the way you just ran off the other—"

"You gotta get outta here." Blaze appeared from nowhere, heading right for Garrett. My eyes were wide as I watched Garrett shove at Blaze, still trying to come to me.

"Tell him to knock this shit off," Garrett demanded, his focus still on me.

My lips parted as if I was about to speak, but nothing came out. All I could do was just stare back at him; my mind blank as he fought to approach me.

"You're making a scene, Garrett," Blaze continued as a couple of other officers joined him, one of them being Sheriff Myers.

"Come on, son," he said in a low voice. "You've had too much to drink."

"Let's all just stay calm and remain in our seats," Pastor Frank's voice said over the microphone. I turned my head to see why he would say such a thing, but the answer was right in front of my face.

"Disrespectful asshole!" Lucas Armitage shouted, storming toward the chaos with his fists in the air. People were jumping to their feet to get a better view, but I stayed frozen at the end of the pew, finding it hard to breathe.

Oh no.

"Go back to your seat," Blaze warned him as Sheriff Myers and another deputy were nearly dragging Garrett out. "You don't want to do anything. Show some respect to your ex-wife and her family."

"Like you're one to talk," he barked back, though he did slow down.

The doors of the sanctuary slammed as Garrett was finally on the other side, leaving Blaze standing in the gap between Lucas and the exit. The tension in the room felt palpable as Lucas finally spun back around and headed back to his seat. However, though the chaos might've receded, everyone's necks were still craned in one direction.

Right at me.

I swallowed hard, catching Blaze's expressionless face as he headed back to his post. He shook his head when he caught my eye, and I wasn't sure whether to be offended or thankful that he was quick to shut Garrett's advances down. After all, Garrett probably just saw me as a familiar face... right?

I sat through the rest of the service in a numb state, refusing to even try to process what the hell had just happened. I mean, honestly, Garrett was just so drunk that he had no idea what he was doing. But still, he mentioned us not finishing our chat, and maybe it was just my paranoia, but if that didn't catch the nosy Nancys of the town's attention, then I wasn't sure what would.

My mouth felt like I had eaten an entire tub of cotton balls as I stood to my feet, turning to my mom. "We're not staying for the lunch, right?"

"Oh, no way," Mom said quickly, shooing me out of the pew and into the sea of people. "We need to just get you out of here. You're sweating bullets."

"Am I?" I questioned, running my hand along my forehead. Sure enough, my fingers came back glistening with sweat. I had opted for a sleeveless black blouse and dark wash skinny jeans for the funeral, but apparently it hadn't been breathable enough.

"Mrs. Young," a woman's voice called from behind us as we made it to the double doors.

"Oh, Brittany," Mom greeted, pausing off to the side to prevent holding up the traffic of people. "How have you been?"

I took a step toward the door, thinking I would just meet her at the truck, but she stopped me. Her hand grabbed my wrist, tugging me back to her side.

"I've been better," she replied. I finally put a face to the voice, surprised at the woman standing there. She had dark, luscious wavy hair that cascaded down her back. She was wearing a black tea dress, perfectly fitted at the waist. "It was just downright embarrassing of Garrett to come stumbling drunk in here like that." She dabbed a tissue at the corner of her smoky gray eyes. "He'd been doing so much better, you know. We've really been praying for him." Brittany choked up at the end, waving her hand at her face like she was trying not to sob.

"I've been praying for him. I can't imagine how hard this has been for you. Oh, also, this is my daughter, Beth," Mom said, gesturing to me. "She came back for Brad's funeral, but I didn't have a chance to introduce you two."

"Nice to meet you, Beth," Brittany said, extending her manicured hand. "I've heard so much about you. I'm in your mom's Bible study."

Of course, you are.

"That's great," I forced a chipper voice. "Last name is Myers, right?" I ignored the warning glance that Mom shot me as Brittany's smile wavered. Mom had always thought I was too forward.

"It was Myers, yes. It's back to my maiden name, actually, which is Romano."

I nodded but didn't get a chance to say anything as Ty

Miller, one of the men that Sarah had listed off as having dated stepped up to the circle. His dark eyes met mine for a moment, but a moment was all it took to know that he was judging me. Ty's thin lips turned down; his face full of disgust before turning to Brittany. "We need to get over to help serve."

"Oh, of course," she said quickly. "I just wanted to stop and check on Andrea."

"Well, thank you." Mom smiled. "Keep y'all's heads up."

"Will do. Again, nice to meet you, Beth." Brittany gave me a slight nod before falling in step with Ty and filtering out of the church.

I shook my head, following the trail of people. The air felt stale in the foyer, and I didn't slow down as I pushed through the front glass doors. I welcomed the heat of the day, but also, part of me wondered if Garrett was still out there...

"I don't know why you have to be so cold," Mom grumbled beside me.

I ignored the comment, deciding Garrett in his current state wouldn't be helpful anyway. Taking a breath, I headed toward the truck, Mom in tow. My heels clicked obnoxiously on the pavement as I rounded the corner to the side lot, Mom's silver half-ton in sight. However, just as I did, I caught sight of the U.S. Marshal on the phone.

"Shoulda been there," he chuckled. "The high-class

defense attorney was there, too. Right in the middle of the drama." My face went hot as I ducked past him, his words ceasing as he saw us.

"Slow down," Mom huffed behind me. "Jeez."

"Sorry," I muttered as I reached the driver's side door. "That was insane."

Mom laughed. "You just ain't been home in a while."

CHAPTER ELEVEN

I stood there, watching the sun set across the rolling fields of the ranch. Orange and pink hues painted the skies, complementing the lingering green of the grasses, dotted with horses and cattle. There were so many good memories from my childhood, riding and working cattle with my dad and brother. Yet somehow, I struggled to recall anything before that May of my senior year. I wanted to move past what happened to Sam, and honestly, I had accepted the fact that he was gone...

It was just the bitterness that lingered. And that was on me, I knew that.

Letting out a sigh, I glanced back over my shoulder, my mom's silhouette visible through the kitchen window. She was cleaning up from a silent dinner between the two of us. Things had been strained for a long time, though I had to admit that maybe I was starting to understand her a little better. She was just doing the best she could in the world she was raised in—and never left.

Just as I considered going inside, I saw a sheriff deputy's truck pulling up to the barn apartment, and my heart stuttered as I saw Blaze get out of the driver's side door. I brushed off the reaction, deeming it solely because he was my inside source into the investigation. I took off down the porch steps, waving my arm like a giddy schoolgirl.

Yikes.

"Blaze!" I huffed as I made it to the barn, catching him at the bottom of the apartment stairs.

"You, okay?" He raised a peculiar eyebrow at me, pausing with one foot on the bottom step.

"Anything come of the funeral?" I asked, still trying to catch my breath. *I should really workout.*

"What do you mean? If you ask me, you would know just as well as I would about the whole funeral." He chuckled, shaking his head, though there was something off in his voice.

"Yeah, I know about the whole drunk Garrett incident, I just was wondering how the case was going, I guess." I shrugged, trying to be nonchalant about it, but my heart was racing.

"Beth..." his voice trailed off as he glanced up the stairs, before letting out an audible breath and turning back to me. "I don't think I should be sharing any information with you."

"What, why?" I demanded, offense filling my voice.

"Well, for starters, we're still not sure if you or Garrett were the last person to see Sarah. On top of that, your alibi is not exactly rock solid, Beth. You seem to have a grudge against this town, too."

My mouth dropped open. "Are you kidding me right now?"

"Listen," Blaze put his hands up in some sort of surrender gesture. "I don't know what you want me to say. You're a criminal defense attorney for heaven's sake. You know as good as I do that things aren't always black and white with these cases. We can't rule anyone —"

"Just stop." I shook my head at him. "I can't believe you actually think that I could be involved." I turned to go, my chest burning with frustration.

This is ridiculous.

He grabbed my wrist before I made it too far, his grip startling me. "Don't go running off like that."

I ripped my arm away. "What the hell do you expect me to do when you're accusing me of killing someone? I didn't have anything to do with Sarah's murder. I want answers, just like you. That's it. I feel horrible over what happened...like why didn't I go after her when she cut out and said she had to go to the restroom? I knew something was up," I continued, my voice straining as the guilt returned. "And why didn't I look harder for her? Why didn't I call the police? I mean, yeah, I had no idea what she was doing or where she was going, but I knew that something was wrong with the way her phone was blowing up."

Blaze's face softened. "We haven't been able to find

her phone and still are waiting for the documents from the phone company…and for the record," he hesitated for a second. "I don't think you did it. I just have to be careful. There're some things that aren't making a lot of sense."

"Like the fact that Sheriff Myers failed to report that I saw Garrett in the same area as Sarah would've been?"

He shrugged. "I don't know. There's also the estranged relationship that she had with Lucas. Something is fishy with that whole mess. I know that Lucas is involved in some shady shit that happens around here but that doesn't make him a murderer. There's also Ty Miller, too. No one can account for him. But there's also… more."

"Like what?" I narrowed my eyes at him.

"I can't tell you all the shit we're investigating, Beth. You know that, and as much as I respect you, I need to walk the straight and narrow on this." The way he said the last bit caused me pause, but I ignored it.

"I get it," I said, forcing a somewhat pleasant smile. "I know that you have to keep it confidential."

"Yeah." His voice had a hint of defeat in it. "I'm sorry."

"It's okay. Have a good night." I turned to go.

"You want a beer or something?" he called after me.

"Not tonight. I have some things to do." I didn't look back at him as I answered, continuing in the direction of the house. As I climbed the steps to the porch, the door opened, Mom walking out.

"What's up?" she asked, a nosy grin on her face. "I saw you talking to Blaze."

I laughed. "It's not what you're thinking, Mom. I'm not in the place to start a new relationship, but I can appreciate your matchmaking skills. Blaze isn't the worst."

Her eyes lit up in a way that stirred my chest. "Maybe in time then."

"Maybe." I had to give it to her. "I think I'm going to go for a drive if that's okay. I'll be back in a little while."

Mom gave me a funny look. "Is everything okay?"

"Um, well, I mean, there's just been a lot going on since I came home. Losing Dad was hard enough, but all this with Sarah... I don't know. I just think I need to get out for a while."

"Okay." She nodded. "Just be careful, okay?"

My heart squeezed at the worry in her voice. "Always. You don't have to worry."

"I will anyway. It seems like the whole town has lost their minds. I saw in the paper that they're wanting to change the curfew for the young people to be home by ten instead of eleven."

I raised my eyebrows. "I think everyone is just shaken up over what happened. It's probably an isolated event, but it's a normal knee-jerk reaction to something terrible." She nodded as I reached inside the door to grab the truck keys from the hook. "Everything will be all right, Mom." I said the words like I meant them because

I did.

She gave me a soft and short hug. "Love you, Beth."

"Love you." I took off down the steps, heading toward the old blue truck parked out by Blaze's. He was nowhere in sight, thankfully, which meant I could leave without him asking any questions, not that he would.

I unlocked the driver's side door and slid in, starting the engine. The truck was louder than most, and I had always been able to recognize the distinct sound when my dad would come into town to pick up Sam and me from school. I backed out and headed down the gravel driveway. I took a right instead of left, heading down the road that led to Hollow Creek Bridge.

I just wanted to see it for myself.

CHAPTER TWELVE

The bridge stood out, just as it always had. Radiused steel loomed multiple feet into the sky, while weathered wood made for the flooring. I pulled off to the side of the road, camouflaging myself in a thicket of trees. I put the truck in park and killed the engine. The sun was nearly gone beneath the horizon, and as much as I didn't want to admit it, there was an eerie feeling hanging over me as I pushed open the truck door.

Why the hell am I here?

The question bounced around in my head as if it were a red flag that I should take heed of as a warning—but I ignored it, shutting the door softly. Heart racing, I made it to the edge of the bridge, where the gravel transitioned to wood. My boots made a hollow thud as I walked along, disrupting the quiet of the evening. I came to stop in the center, peering over the rails.

I don't know why I thought I needed to do that. There was nothing there to see. Nothing was left, not even the crime scene tape that had been shown on the news.

My stomach lurched as I thought of Sarah all those feet down, discarded like trash. Tears threatened to well up in my eyes and I pushed them away. The site was less than a mile from where Garrett had wrecked his truck that night with Sam and me as passengers.

It's just a coincidence.

Honestly, I knew that it was. A car accident wouldn't have any relation to a murder, not these many years apart. I mean, yeah, I had been at Sarah's graduation party that night and had chosen to leave early. I felt out of place there after my best friend, Lauren, had left.

Lauren.

That was someone I hadn't talked to since that night. Last I had heard, she was out in California, pursuing some crazy dream of being an actress. I nearly laughed to myself, thinking of how dreamy the notion seemed. Back when I was younger—before the crash—I wouldn't have thought it to be unreasonable. I was like everyone else in the town, dying to get out and make a name for themselves. But that's the thing about small towns, a person grows up with the small-minded notion that somehow, they'll stand out in the sea of people.

But it's not easy, and the sea is much bigger than anyone can wrap their mind around.

Resigning to the fact that the visit had done nothing for me, I turned to go, making my way back to the truck. The last little bit of light from the sun was cutting through the thick woods at the edge of the drop off to the creek, still overgrown but trampled. Just as I reached for the door handle, my eye caught something off in the grass, glimmering under the slightest bit of illumination.

What the hell?

I squinted, keeping my eyes focused on the glimmer, trudging into the thorn bushes. The thorns tore at my jeans, but I ignored them as I finally realized what I was staring at.

No freaking way.

My eyes were locked onto a cell phone, screen pointed upward. It was halfway covered with dirt, as if it had hit the ground with some impact. The screen was shattered, but the outside case, pink leopard print, made my hands go numb.

"How did they miss this?" I mumbled to myself, stopping myself before I leaned over to pick it up. *Wait!* I knew better than to do that. Instead, I pulled my own phone from my pocket, scrolling to Blaze's number, which my mother had urged me to put in my contact list.

Glad I did.

I hit the call and put it up to my ear, eerily looking around myself.

"Beth?" Blaze answered, his voice groggy like he had been sleeping.

"Hi to you, too," I chuckled. "I need you to come down to Hollow Creek Bridge, like right now."

He was silent for a second. "What the hell are you doing down there, Beth? If someone sees you, they're going to think it's suspicious. That's not a good look for you."

"Yeah, thanks, Mom. Can you get down here pronto? I found Sarah's phone."

"No way." I could hear rustling in the background and then doors slamming. "I'm on my way. You need to wait in the truck and lock the doors. I don't like you being down in that area alone."

I fought the urge to roll my eyes at him. "Got it, but just don't tell Mom, okay? She'll freak out worse than you are right now."

"Won't tell a soul if you get in the truck and lock the doors."

That time I did roll my eyes. "Cool, whatever." I turned around and jerked the handle before climbing into the driver's side seat. I shut and locked the doors. "I followed your instructions, now you don't have to tell anyone."

"Okay, good. I'm already on my way, anyway."

Suddenly, the hair on the back of my neck raised, a shudder running down my spine as the silence surrounded me. I sat still, listening as the crickets ceased to chirp.

"Beth?" Blaze's voice filled my ear.

Just then, I saw headlights appear in the distance. "Are you almost here?"

"No..."

"So, these aren't your headlights?"

"Just stay in the truck." His voice had an air of warning.

I kept my eyes focused on the lights, appearing to slow down as a truck bumped over the bridge.

Please don't notice me.

My skin prickled with anticipation as the dark-colored truck inched forward, the lights switching from low-beam to high-beam, blinding me. I wasn't sure if it was a sign that they had noticed something in the trees... Or if it was just a coincidence.

Holding my breath, I waited for them to pass me, giving me a chance to peer through the passenger side window. However, just as their lights passed the front of my truck, they stomped the gas, speeding away too fast to give me a view.

"What the hell," I grumbled to myself. I was left in a dark cloud of dust, hardly able to comprehend what had just taken place. The hair on the back of my neck settled as the taillights faded into the ever-growing blackness, and I glanced down, seeing the call-failed notification on the screen.

"Well, I guess it's a good thing that didn't turn into an emergency," I said with a sigh, sitting my phone down on the console. I leaned back in the seat, resting my head against the worn leather. I sat like that for a few moments before a second set of headlights came pouring into my vision. This vehicle was moving about ten times as fast as the last.

Blaze's truck came to a skidding stop just outside of mine, his door slinging open. "Beth!"

I opened my door, peering over to him. "All is good," I called to him, noticing that his gun was drawn from his belt. "Just a passerby."

I think.

There was a good chance I had just read too much into the occurrence. This road was travelled more often than most thought, since it did lead to quite a few farms in the area.

He put away his gun. "Where's the phone?" Blaze asked, clicking on his flashlight, an evidence bag in his other hand.

I shut the truck door before motioning to the general area. "It's partially covered in dirt. I don't know how your guys missed it, honestly."

"Well, we're not exactly top of the line detectives," he grunted as he leaned over and scooped it up into the bag. "You probably knew that though."

"Yeah, but shouldn't the state be helping out?"

"Sheriff Myers hasn't asked for their assistance." Blaze tried to turn the phone on through the plastic bag. "Dead. Figures."

"What about the U.S. Marshal then?" I couldn't hold back the burning question. "I saw him at the funeral."

And heard him talking about me.

"Oh, you mean Daniel Marlow. Yeah, he's here on other business."

"I won't ask what business that is," I said with a sigh, somewhat disappointed as I watched Blaze set the phone into the back seat of his truck. Part of me was regretting turning it in so fast, instead of charging the battery and scrolling through it myself. Then again, it was probably passcode protected.

"I wouldn't tell you what business," he quipped, chuckling. "But really, what the hell were you doing out here? You don't need to be running around like this. Nothing good is gonna come of it. It's not just that it might cause people to talk, either, it could be dangerous for all we know. It's not like we know who did this, and not to freak you out, but there is evidence of a serial killer lurking around these parts."

I narrowed my eyes. "A serial killer, huh?"

"Yeah," he gave me a face. "You should be careful. You fit the profile of his victims."

"And what is that profile, Blaze?" I joked. "Smart, sassy, and—"

"Twenties and thirties, slender, and pretty...typically with dark or reddish hair," he cut me off, pursing his lips. "I'm not making jokes."

My gut clenched at the serious look on his face. "Oh, sorry."

"They're calling him the Back Road Phantom."

"Some name," I muttered, running my fingers through my hair damp with sweat. "I guess I'll stay off dark back roads from now on."

"Probably a good idea."

CHAPTER THIRTEEN

I knew that I should've gone home, but Blaze had taken off toward the Sheriff's office, and I still hadn't done what I had intended to do—besides seeing Hollow Creek Bridge. I gunned the engine of the truck down Main Street before pulling into the parking lot of Outlaws. I had one intention, find Garrett. Granted, he would more than likely be drunk, but I had to try and talk to him. Even if the idea left my stomach nauseous.

Smoothing out my hair, I dabbed the sweat from my face. I looked like a bit of a wreck, but I was pretty certain that it wasn't a new look in this town. I slid out of the truck and headed inside, noting that there was no one standing outside like there had been before. I pushed through the saloon-style doors, the smoky haze immediate as I took a few steps into the entrance. The guy there didn't even give me a second look as I made my way toward the bar, figuring liquid courage might not be such a bad idea.

"What can I get for you, Beth?" the woman behind the bar asked me, her use of my name a little startling.

"Um," I paused. "Do I know you?" I took in her dark hair, piled on top of her head in a messy bun. She had on a tight white T-shirt that accentuated her large chest and tiny waist. I still didn't recognize her.

"Really?" she raised her brows. "It's me! Lauren!"

My mouth dropped open as I met those familiar amber eyes. "Oh my gosh. I am so sorry, Lauren. Your hair was always blonde, and..." my eyes dropped to her chest. "I don't... those..."

"Are fake," she laughed, shaking her head at me. "I got them thinking they'd help me make it out in Los Angeles. It turns out that everyone has them there."

I joined her laughter. "I can only imagine, but seriously," my laugh faded. "What're you doing back in town? I thought you had moved and would never come back."

"Ah, yeah, those were the days," she said with a sigh. "What do you want to drink? I feel like you need it more than I do tonight. You look exhausted."

"Just a Jack and Coke will do."

"Single or double?"

"Single," I answered as she started making my drink. "So, what's up with you?"

"Well, I have a five-year-old daughter, Bria," she began as she made the drink. "Her dad is some high-class talent agent out in LA. He pays a monthly stipend of child support, but that's the extent of his involvement. Other than that, I moved home because I was tired of the fast life. I guess it turns out that I belong here." She sat my drink down in front of me. "But given how crazy things are here, I don't know if it's much better."

"I hear that."

"Why're you here?" she asked, leaning against the bar across from me. "I didn't think you'd ever come back to this place."

"My dad passed," I said softly, still getting used to the idea that he was gone. My mind might be overwhelmed and laser-focused on Sarah, but the grief still felt like a ton of bricks.

"Oh shit," she gasped. "I am so sorry. I had no idea. I don't read the paper or anything. I try to just stay the hell out of it. I only knew about Sarah's murder because of how much people talk in here. That and she's a pretty big regular, always entertaining some new guy."

"Some things never change, I guess."

"Oh, I know, right? Not to speak ill of the dead, but seriously, any time that she and Lucas had a bad spell, even after they were married, she'd be out surveying the town without her wedding ring. She is…well, *was* a mess."

"And yet the men still flocked to her," I chuckled, taking a long sip of the bittersweet drink. I was thankful that Lauren wasn't prying about the past or the fact that I ghosted her after the accident. So, I gathered up the nerve to ask the hard question. "Have you seen Garrett around tonight?"

"Garrett Myers?" Her voice was tinged with curiosity.

"Yeah, that Garrett." I tried to stay nonchalant in my delivery, but my voice still came out strained.

"Um well, you know..." her voice trailed off as she scanned the crowd. "He usually is here every single night that we're open, but he hasn't been here tonight."

"Does he usually stumble around out back?"

She laughed, though there wasn't much humor to it. "The guy stumbles around everywhere. Apparently, he's been like that since... Well, you know."

I nodded, shifting on the bar stool as I forced myself to stay in the uncomfortable conversation. "I've heard similar things. He's been wanting to talk to me, and um, I just thought..."

"I heard about what happened at the funeral," she commented, her eyes dropping to her clasped hands on the bar. "I think that's pretty terrible that he came storming in there looking for you."

Looking for me?

"I don't think he was looking for me," I countered quickly. "I think I was just the first familiar face that he saw."

She shrugged. "I don't know. That's just the rumor floating around town. You know how people talk. I don't ever really take people for their word, honestly. I hear the wildest shit...though I do know something..."

Lauren chewed her plump red lip.

"What's that?" I downed the rest of my drink.

"So, I only know this for sure because Sarah got really drunk here one night…the night she found out, actually."

"What did she find out?"

"She was pregnant."

My mouth dropped open. "But she drank the night that we came here," I reasoned, shaking my head. "That doesn't make any sense at all."

"Well, I mean, not everyone listens to the doctor's guidance," she laughed. "There are plenty of women who do a lot of dumb things when they're pregnant. She showed me the test, so I know that it's the truth. I don't know what she did about it after the fact, though."

"Who was the dad?"

She gave me a funny look. "Only God knows. Like I said, she's always entertained a ton of men around here. The decent ones tend to cut and run early, but even then, there's something about her that just draws them in, ya know? She was beautiful and sweet, and probably a little naïve in the way that she was so trusting. But in my opinion, you never really know someone. That's the LA experience talking."

I nodded in agreement, though I was still stunned by the news. I wasn't going to pass judgment on Sarah for how she chose to live or date or who she slept with, but it only added more mystery to the *who*, behind all those phone calls. "Do you know who she was seeing most recently?"

"You sound like the cops," Lauren quipped. "But, um, to answer the question, the most recent person I saw her with would've been Blaze Harris, though I know that never amounted to anything. And then Ty Miller. Garrett was always around her, too. I'm sure that he had a thing for her, but who knows when it comes to him. My guess is he was too drunk to get it up."

"Gotcha," I said, making a mental note. As much as I hated hearing Blaze's name in the mix, it also made me wonder if there was more to the story than he was telling. And well, Ty Miller had been the one to shout out something at the funeral. Had he been interviewed?

I'm starting to take this whole thing too seriously. I'm not a detective. But at the same time, I felt desperate for answers.

"Hey, here's my number," Lauren said, scribbling on a napkin. "I need to get back to customers but call me sometime. I'd love to catch up with you. Hear some stories about the Windy City."

"Yeah, of course," I said, though Lauren was already gone, heading off to speak with a customer flagging her down. I grabbed up the napkin, shoving it into my jeans pocket before heading for the back exit—the same one that I had gone out of the last time.

No one seemed to notice as I disappeared down the dimly lit hallway, slipping out of the door and into the night air. Surprisingly, this time the motion lights immediately kicked on, illuminating the very empty gravel area. There wasn't a soul in sight, and while I was disappointed to not see Garrett, part of me was also relieved. My boots crunched on the gravel as I made my way back around to the parking lot.

But then something caught my attention.

The door of my truck was *wide* open.

My heart jumped to my throat as I stood there frozen, wondering if I had been careless enough to leave it open or if someone else had done it. I inched toward the truck, halfway prepared for someone to jump out of nowhere and grab me, the serial killer coming back to mind. I lunged for the door, peering inside for split second before shutting myself inside. I took a deep breath as I hit the lock button, gazing around to see if anything had been stolen.

It looked clear. Until I caught sight of a piece of paper sitting in the passenger seat.

Go back to where you came from Beth or else.

CHAPTER FOURTEEN

"I don't know," Blaze said, staring down at the note the following afternoon, which was now in an evidence bag. "It could just be someone doesn't want you in town."

"Really?" I snapped, shaking my head. "So, this is just some weird coincidence then?"

He threw his hands up as I stood inside the entryway of his apartment. "I don't know. I mean, I'll take it down to the station, but that's the best I can do. I don't know if Sheriff Myers will want to do anything with it."

"Well, you could test it for prints or something."

"Yeah, because our department has so much excess funding." He sounded annoyed with me, though his eyes told a different story—looking more fatigued than anything. The guy had a lot on his plate, and I was certain in the moment, I wasn't doing much to help. "But I'll do what I can, okay? And seriously, would you just stay the hell at home? Your mom needs you, and you have the shit to work out with the ranch. Maybe you should focus on that instead of playing amateur detective. You've already got the entire town's eyes on you."

I sighed, thinking maybe he was right—even though it went against the grain. "I guess it's just bothering me."

"I understand." He gave me a sympathetic look. "But your guilt or curiosity, whatever is making you feel like you need to dig, is just making it harder for everyone else. And by everyone else, I mean your mom. Like come on, the woman has lost her son and her husband. I'd hate to see her lose you, too."

"Yeah, okay," I reluctantly sighed. "I'll finish up all the affairs with the ranch, and then maybe just see where I'm at."

"You're putting it off, aren't you?"

I hesitated, thinking of the payments that I had yet to make. "I don't know."

"You don't really wanna leave town." His eyes leveled with me in a way that made my stomach flutter. I became immensely aware of how alone we were.

"Sheriff Myers told me to stay around town," I choked out, taking a step back in hopes that it would relieve some of the tension building between us.

"Come on," Blaze chuckled. "We both know that's not why you're still here."

I pursed my lips, already knowing deep down that he was right. I was struggling to come to terms with it. "I don't know. But I'll stop with everything."

"Yeah, you're starting to act like all the other people who live here. You know, the ones who go sticking their nose into everything."

I narrowed my eyes at him. "You're ridiculous."

"Just calling it like I see it, darlin'."

I rolled my eyes and spun around, hating the way his deep southern draw got to me. I ripped the apartment door open and went storming down the steps. *What's that verse say in the Bible? Something about fleeing from temptation.* And that's exactly what Blaze was to me.

I stepped out into the late-afternoon sun, the heat less suffocating than usual. However, the sight of a red truck pulling into the driveway caused me to stop. I waited where I was as they parked next to my dad's old Ford. Nothing about the truck was familiar, but the person who appeared from the driver's seat was.

"Hey, Beth," Garrett greeted me, his eyes clear beneath his faded ballcap. He was in a black T-shirt and jeans, and honestly, he looked so much like the younger version of himself, that it made my chest feel a little tight. "I was hoping I'd find you here."

"Well, I do live here now," I answered awkwardly, shifting my weight into the heels of my boots. "Is there something I can do for you?"

"Uh... yeah... kind of... I don't know." The way he was stumbling over his words might've made someone think that he was still drunk, but I could tell from the strain in his voice it was purely emotion.

I looked back up at the apartment, where I knew Blaze was, and the fact he was there provided some sort of security. "Do you wanna talk?"

"Actually, I came here to apologize for what happened at Sarah's funeral. I don't even remember it, but I heard it was really bad. It's really knocked my head for a loop that you're back in town. I ain't seen you since, well, you know." He cleared his throat, and in the moment I felt the pain in his voice. "And about that, too, I'm still paying for what happened that night…and not in the sense of probation or whatever, because they dropped the manslaughter charges."

"I know," I said, my voice coming out flat, while my insides were spinning with a heavy load of sadness. I never saw Garrett after the crash. He'd been booked on manslaughter charges and thrown into the county jail. He wasn't able to make the funeral for Sam. About that same time, I went off to college, and never really came back.

"Yeah, I just wanted to tell you that I still think about him," Garrett's voice was thickening. "And I think that's my punishment for surviving."

Something in my chest did a one-eighty as his words hit home. "You've punished yourself enough," I caught myself saying, the bitterness seeping from my body. "And I… I forgive you. I'm sorry for avoiding you all these years…I just… I hated coming home, you know?"

He nodded, and I swore the relief was visible

throughout his whole body. "I loved you, Beth. I really did, and I loved your brother, too. I'll never stop hating myself for what happened."

"We were young and dumb," I said, clearing my throat in an attempt to rid the lump growing. "The past is the past, and I think it's about time that we both let it go."

A slight smile tugged at his lips. "So, I guess you've been hanging on to it, too, then? Good to know that I'm not so alone."

"Yeah, something like that," I admitted, suddenly realizing just how lonely I had been living over the past sixteen years.

"Also, um," he hesitated, looking around us. "I think... I think you're in danger."

"What?"

Just as he opened his mouth to speak, Blaze cut him off. "What the hell are you doing here, Garrett? Was the scene in the middle of the church not enough for you?"

"Wait," I called out as Blaze stormed past me, shooing Garrett toward his truck. "Stop!"

Blaze ignored me. "Get the hell off this property, man. No one wants you here. You've done enough to Beth."

"Dude, I was just here to apologize," Garrett fought back, gesturing past Blaze to me.

"He's fine, Blaze, let him be," I ordered, but it was as if Blaze didn't hear me at all. "We were just talking—"

"Listen to her," Garrett shouted, just before shoving at Blaze's chest.

"She has no idea what you are," Blaze roared as he shoved him into the side of the truck. "Get out of here!"

Garrett looked completely unfazed by the violence, shaking his head as he jumped into the driver's seat. His eyes locked with mine. "I meant what I said, Beth." With that, he slammed the door and gunned the truck backwards, leaving me there with the disgruntled ranch manager. And to say Blaze was pissed would be an understatement.

"I told you to stay out of all this!" He spun around, his anger focused on me now. "I don't understand why that's so hard for you to do."

"What are you talking about?" I retorted, folding my arms across my chest. I was used to men who had tempers, and I didn't play into the intimidation. "He showed up here all on his own."

"Yeah, because you're being so damn nosy," he snapped, taking a step toward me. "You come into this town after how many years of being gone? Ten? Twelve? Or is it more like sixteen? I mean, yeah, I heard you used to roll in here for a day or two on the holidays, but that shit doesn't count."

"Who are you to come at me with this? You're not from here. You weren't even around back when I left town."

"No, you're right. I wasn't. I just had to listen to your

parents live a life in nothing but grief. They lost two of their kids that night. You left the moment you could, and you never came back. You might as well have been dead, too."

Hurt seared through my chest as I suddenly noticed my mom standing on the back porch, her brows furrowed. I parted my lips to say something as I turned back to Blaze, tears blurring my vision.

"Yeah, you don't have anything to say to that, do you?" His words were sharp and callous as I dug the keys from my pocket, having had enough of the conversation.

"Beth, wait!" Mom called from the porch as I ripped the door open of the blue Ford. "We never thought—"

The engine cut off her voice and I slammed the door shut, barely letting it latch before I put it in reverse. I had no idea where I was going but I knew who I needed to find.

CHAPTER FIFTEEN

I sped down the highway, Blaze's harsh words reverberating in my mind. I mean, yeah, there was some truth to them. However, I'd also always called home multiple times a week. My parents knew what was going on in my life, even if I wasn't there. I went home for holidays the best I could, given my work schedule, and if I couldn't make it, I always flew my parents to me.

So, what was it with Blaze? Was it really me? Or was it Garrett that made him so angry?

There was no way to know what the real answer was as I pulled into the bar parking lot, searching for the red truck that I assumed was Garrett's. I didn't see it immediately, but it didn't stop me from parking and heading in.

"Hey," Lauren greeted me, her dark hair in loose waves this time. "You look... mad?"

I shook my head. "I don't know what I am at the moment." I glanced around the mostly empty place, disappointment filling my chest. I turned back to

Lauren, who was already pouring a drink for me. "Have you seen Garrett?"

"Do you always just wander around town looking for him?" She smirked. "If I didn't know better, I'd be thinking that the two of you have something going on. I know you had a serious crush on him in high school."

"Did I?" I chuckled. "I don't remember that." Well, I did remember that—but it was a distant memory. "He stopped by the house, and I was kind of thinking he might've come here."

"No, he hasn't been here in a couple days, like I told you. He goes through these spurts of trying to sober up, and if it were my guess, I'd say that's what he's doing. That's the only time he misses a night here."

I picked up the drink, gulping it down like it was water. "So, you weren't working the night I was here with Sarah?"

"No, I actually only work a few nights a week," Lauren answered, giving me a curious look. "You would've seen me here. And if you didn't, I definitely would've sought you out."

"Of course," I said, giving her a smile. I took a seat on the bar stool, forcing myself to take a deep breath. "I swear, coming back to this town has been so... surreal."

She gave me a sympathetic look. "I can only imagine, but... well..." her voice trailed off for a brief moment. "If you don't mind me asking, why are you looking for Garrett?"

"We were just in the middle of a conversation when Blaze ran him off," I said, not wanting to include the fact that Garrett said I was in danger and I wanted to know why.

"So... I take it you've made peace with him then?" Her words sounded cautious, like I might explode on her.

I sighed, the burden I'd been carrying on my shoulders was not nearly as heavy as it was before. "Yeah, I hadn't talked to him since it all happened, and maybe I was unfair for being so unforgiving toward him."

She gave me a smile. "That's good, Beth. I'm happy for you. And I'm sorry I ghosted you the way I did the summer after our senior year. I just... You were so bitter and angry. I understood, but it was hard to be around you."

"Wait, I thought I ghosted you?" I gave her a look, setting my drink back down.

"Wait, did you ghost me?" She burst into a fit of laughter. "Well, whatever happened between us is water under the bridge. I'm ready to move on from it."

"Me, too," I agreed, leaning against the bar.

"Are you gonna stay around?" Lauren asked, grabbing up a stool from the other side and taking a seat across from me. "Because I'm not gonna lie, it would be nice to have you stay."

"Well, I'm draining my life savings to pay off most of the ranch's debt, so I doubt I'll be going far. It'll take some time to rebuild, and I don't know..." my voice trailed off as I thought of my mom. "I could probably stand to work on things with Mom. She's always just wanted what was best for me," I laughed. "Even if it means she plays matchmaker all the time."

"Ooh, girl, she was doing that in high school, too," Lauren giggled. "I guess some things never change, huh? Who is it now?"

"Blaze," I answered her, though I no longer felt a jitter of excitement when I said his name. Something about the way he portrayed himself toward Garrett had me questioning his character.

"He is pretty hot," Lauren commented. "But I don't see him as being your type. He's got an interesting past."

"What kind of past?" I hesitated, tilting my head at her.

"I don't know, exactly," she answered. "I heard he's been with a lot of women, and that he's got a fighting side."

"So typical cowboy then."

"Exactly," she teased. "Want another one?"

Before I could answer her, my phone rang, buzzing in my jeans pocket. I dug it out, half expecting to see Blaze or Mom's name on the screen.

But it was neither.

"Who is that?" Lauren asked, having probably noticed the confused look on my face.

"I don't know, but it's our area code…" I hit the answer button, taking the risk. "Hello?"

"Is this Beth?" a frantic female voice came over the line.

"Um, yeah…" my voice trailed off. "Can I help you?"

"This is Brittany, Garrett's wife…ex-wife…I… I can't find Garrett." The panic in her voice was palpable as she spoke. "Is he with you? The last time we talked, he said he was going to see you."

"No, he's not with me," I admitted. "He came out to the ranch but then left. I actually came into town looking for him, but he's not anywhere around here…at least not at Outlaws."

"Oh my gosh, I knew it," she cried, a sobbing noise coming from over the phone. "I keep an app on his phone because sometimes he goes on binges, and I've been tracking it because he's been drinking so heavily lately. I thought he turned it off, but it shows his last location was at Hollow Creek Bridge and I just know he's going to do something, Beth, I know he is."

"I… I don't think I understand," I muttered as I slid off the stool and gave Lauren a small wave. "What do you mean?"

"Beth, he was the father of Sarah's baby," she sobbed, her breathy cries filling my ears. "I know you meant so much to him, can you please help me look for him? I've already called his dad."

"Okay, okay," I said quickly, picking up into a jog as I

headed back to the truck. "I'll help you look for him."

"Meet me at the bridge?" she offered. "I just know something is wrong. So many people are angry with him, and they all think he did it, but he didn't. I know he didn't."

"Yeah, I know." I started the engine, trying to process what I could potentially be driving up on. "I'll meet you there."

"Thank you so much, Beth," Brittany said, still audibly crying. "Thank you."

***

I stared at the road ahead of me as I headed out of town, a sinking feeling in my stomach. I felt like I was missing something, like there was a piece of the puzzle right in front of my face that wasn't making any sense.

Was Garrett coming to make things right before he said his own goodbyes?

That's how Brittany had made it sound on the phone… Or was she worried Garrett was up to something much, much worse? I glanced down at my phone in my lap, buzzing again. This time it was Blaze. I ignored it, gunning toward Hollow Creek Bridge.

CHAPTER SIXTEEN

I turned down the road just as the sun sank beneath the horizon, the same timing as I had before. There was something about the timing that stuck out in my brain, but I didn't question it very long, my mind stuck on the horror of what I might find there. However, as I neared the bridge, I didn't see a single vehicle in sight—and I knew there was no way to hide Garrett's red truck.

Just leave it and go home.

But I pushed the warning thought away, pulling off the side of the road and parking—on the opposite side as I had before. That being said, I didn't just jump out of the truck and go poking around. I reached around behind the seat, sticking my hand underneath it. My fingers brushed the cold steel of my dad's old shotgun, and I tugged it out, scooting around a couple of empty bottles of antibiotics. I knew there wasn't one in the chamber as I pulled it over into the front seat with me, but all I'd have to do is rack it—and I'd be good.

Here we go.

I kicked open the driver's side door, and slid out, the air feeling a little cool as it hit me in the face. My nostrils filled with the deep woodsy scent of the brush surrounding me, and it once had been one of my favorite smells. In the moment though, it was hardly comforting. I stood there, just outside of the truck, for a minute or so as the quiet settled in around me. It didn't seem like anyone was there.

Boots thudding across the wooden bridge, I made my way to the railing, my heart racing. I took a deep breath and leaned over, halfway expecting to see something horrifying. However, there was nothing. I peered down, my eyes pouring over the muddy water, a hazy brown color.

Wait a second.

Gun in one hand, I dug my other into my pocket, fishing my phone out. I opened the screen, ignoring the missed calls from Blaze and my mom. I went to my contacts, typing Garrett's name in the search bar. His name instantly popped up, having been kept in the mix of hundreds of names over the years. However, the chances of him having the same number was slim.

Regardless, I hit the call button, putting the phone up to my ear as I gazed back over the guardrail. Something about the whole mess just didn't make sense. The phone rang and rang before going to voicemail.

"You've reached Garrett, leave me a message and I'll get back to you."

My mouth went dry at the sound of his voice.

"Hey, it's Beth. Brittany called and said that you were at the bridge..." my voice trailed off at the sound of tires. "I don't know why I'm calling. Sorry. Um, hope you're okay." Shaking my head at how silly I sounded, I turned back to the noise behind me. Unsurprised, I saw Brittany jumping out of the driver's side of a dark SUV.

"He's not here, is he?" she jogged up to me, her eyes dropping to the gun. "I think he found the app I put on his phone." Her face fell in defeat. "I don't really know how to help him. I try so hard to keep up with him. I know that we're over, but I just keep praying that he'll come back, you know?" She looked back up at me, her eyes brimming with tears.

"Yeah, I get that," I said, my shoulders slumping. "I'm sorry that I couldn't help you, Brittany. I really am. I'm sure he'll show up somewhere..." my voice trailed off as her eyes narrowed at me.

"Do *you* know where he is?" Something in her voice shifted.

"Uh... I do not." I had no idea how to take the way her eyes were darkening, her body tensing up as she blocked the way to my truck.

"Really? Because you're all he's talked about since you showed back up to town. Actually, I guess that wouldn't even be the truth. The man has gabbed about you since I met him. Every time he got drunk, he'd go ranting and raving about needing to tell some bitch named Beth he was sorry."

I raised my eyebrows at her. "My brother was his best

friend."

"How cute," she snapped, her eyes boring into mine. The hair on the back of my neck stood on end as she took a step toward me. "You know what else is cute?"

"What's that?" I choked out, tightening my grip on the gun. I had no idea what level of psycho I was dealing with, but it was quickly escalating past jealous ex-wife.

"The fact that Sarah thought she was going to be the one who changed Garrett," she laughed, shaking her head as she reached into her back pocket. My breath caught when she pulled a pistol out, holding it out at me. "You can drop that," she nodded to my shotgun. "Because I've been dying to talk to someone about what happened."

And she has no intention of letting me live to snitch.

"Okay," I held my hands up as I sat the gun down on the bridge. "There's not one in the chamber anyway." I was going to have to have a different exit strategy, and my mind was already calculating just how far it was to the creek beneath me.

"Yeah, whatever," she snorted. "Anyway, so this bitch thinks that she can change my husband, right? Like she starts calling him up, and trying to convince him to go to treatment, all the while he's still crashing on my couch. I was trying to save my marriage and she was just out there trying to be a Jezebel and steal him away."

I feigned a sympathetic look. The pro to being a lawyer was knowing when to fake it, and right now, my life was on the line. "So, what did he think about it?"

"What did he think?" Brittany scoffed, shaking the gun around in a way that made me nervous. "Let me tell you what he thought. He thought that he was man enough to actually change for her. We all knew it was a lie, but he gave it a shot. A shot that ended with her knocked up."

The wheels in my head were spinning, trying to put the pieces together. "So, Garrett was the one who got Sarah pregnant?"

"Oh, my God, are you seriously this dense? I told you this on the phone. I heard Lauren talking to Sarah at the bar. And yeah, he got her pregnant.. Do I need to explain how babies are made, Beth?" Her voice shrill as she spoke, the end of that gun still waving around in my direction.

I should've put one in the chamber. I could've taken this crazy bitch.

But instead, I only nodded. "Okay, sorry. I'm just trying to keep up."

"Sarah swore that it was Lucas who was the baby's daddy. She swore it all the way to the grave. She said she and Garrett never even slept together. Can you believe she had the balls to say that right to my face? She was just a bold-faced liar."

Yeah, this girl is psycho.

"That's awful," I said, forcing the words out. "So, you killed Sarah?" I couldn't hide the surprise from my voice as I took in the tiny little brunette.

She burst into a fit of sardonic laughter. "You sound so surprised...like what did you think? Garrett did it? There's no way that man could sober up enough to kill someone, and honestly, I was really thinking they'd just play it off as another Back Road Phantom hit, but silly me. I guess he's only into women who look a lot more like you."

"You really think that you're going to drop me dead in the same place as Sarah and it not be connected to her case?"

"Give me your phone," she demanded, pointing to the bulge in my pocket. "I don't give a shit what you say about anything. Us folks around here know that there's a serial killer running around. This time I'll stage it a little better."

"Okay then," I said, digging my phone out of my pocket. I glanced down at the screen, seeing three missed calls from Garrett. I quickly swiped them clear using my thumb.

Maybe he'll be sober enough to call for help.

"So, Sheriff Myers isn't on his way here, is he?" I asked, tossing the phone to Brittany's feet face down, hoping to bust the screen.

"He's under the assumption that his dear boy killed Sarah. I provided him with evidence."

"But he was drunk the night that she was murdered."

"Says you, the only one who puts him at Outlaws. I

saw him by this bridge that night on my way home from my Bible study. Right around ten-thirty. They're gonna arrest him today, I bet."

That's why Blaze wanted Garrett to leave.

"Smart," I commented as she took another step forward, the barrel now much closer than I preferred. I glanced behind her, hearing what I thought might be the distant sound of a vehicle.

"Shit," I heard her grumble as she heard it to. "Climb up on the rail."

"What?"

"Climb up on the rail now or I'll shoot you dead and leave you here in the middle of the road." She lunged forward and stumbled back, climbing up the back of the rails. "Stand at the edge of the wood on the other side.

I reluctantly did as she said, realizing that I was only seconds from causing my mother absolute sadness and that thought alone tore my heart apart. It was one thing to die—I wasn't afraid of that. I just... I didn't want to leave my mom. She deserved a daughter who stayed, who gave her grandchildren and a shoulder to lean on through all the grief she had gone through.

I should've told her I was staying.

I glanced behind me, peering down. It was just a guess as to whether or not I would survive the fall. My vision went hazy, my ears ringing as I braced myself to let go. But the eruption of a gunshot beat me to my release.

CHAPTER SEVENTEEN

I blinked, expecting to feel pain, but as I glanced down to my hands, I realized they were still gripping the rails in the same place they were before. I looked up and across to where Brittany had been standing. She was still there, though she looked even more shocked than I think I was in the moment.

"Put your fucking gun down," Garrett growled, dropping the barrel of the shotgun down from the sky and racking it again. My jaw dropped at sight of him stalking toward Brittany. "Or I'll kill you."

"Might as well just do it," Brittany snorted, keeping the pistol level, still pointed at me, as she eyed Garrett. "We all know that you knocked up Sarah. You were obsessed."

"I *never* slept with her," he snapped at her. "We were just friends."

"That's what men *always* say—and now that Sarah is gone, you've got your eye set on Beth here." Brittany waved the barrel of the gun, startling me all over again.

"I got your voicemail," Garrett said, his face full of grief as he shifted his attention to me. "Beth, I'm so sorry. I can't even express how sorry I am for all the pain I've caused you over the years. I never wanted to ruin your life. And then the moment you come back to town, I did it all over again."

"You don't have to say sorry," I said exasperated, my heart breaking at the pain on his face. "I'm sorry that I held so much unforgiveness toward you, Garrett. We were just kids..."

"Oh, how *sweet,*" Brittany interjected in a sarcastic tone. "Let's all just make up and be friends, never mind the fact that Garrett killed your brother."

"Shut up!" Garrett roared, taking another step toward her.

I could barely breathe as I watched the moments tick by. I *knew* that Brittany was capable of killing me —she had already murdered someone... But was Garrett capable of killing her to save my life if it came down to it? My hands trembled and my heart pounded in my ears as I waited... My life in the hands of someone who I had spent most of my adult life hating.

"You're just a no-good alcoholic," Brittany focused again on him. "And you seriously thought that you could divorce me and find someone else to put up with your shit?"

Garrett shook his head. "I divorced you because you're *insane.*"

Brittany's head tipped back, a laugh filling the air with the ever-growing sound of sirens in the distance. "Fuck you, Garrett." She steadied the gun, and I swallowed hard. "You'll eventually figure out where you belong."

I squeezed my eyes shut, already knowing what was coming next. *This is it.*

"No—"

A shot pierced the night air, and I caught my breath, expecting to feel pain...

But there was nothing, yet again.

My eyes fluttered open as a ragged breath spilled from my lips. Brittany was doubled over, clinging to her blood-soaked shirt. Tears filled my eyes as Garrett headed to her, who collapsed just as one of the sheriff's trucks came skidding to a stop. Blaze and another officer jumped out.

I watched in shock as they shouted at Garrett, telling him to drop his weapon. Before I could even contest it, they were cuffing him, more officers arriving and rushing to Brittany's body. Blaze caught sight of me and came sprinting.

"I'm so sorry for what happened," he huffed, offering me a hand to help me over the railing. "I shouldn't have said all that shit to you, and I didn't mean it, really. I just... I knew that Garrett was behind all this...and look what happened."

"No, no you're wrong," I snapped, avoiding his hand

as I climbed back over the rails on my own. "It was Brittany behind the whole thing."

"What?" He sounded shocked. "There's no way that it was that little thing."

"Yeah, she lured me," I quickly explained, only getting that far as Sheriff Myers approached us. One of the officers was leading Garrett away as he locked eyes with me, mouthing, *"I'm sorry."*

I couldn't contain my emotions in the moment, and the tears flowed freely down my cheeks as I watched the officer stuff him into the back of a police car. He slammed the door and headed over to a few other officers who were standing there in a group.

"I'm really sorry about this," Sheriff Myers said to me, catching my attention. "We just need to get your statement and I'll let ya go home, Beth. I can only imagine how traumatic it was."

Blaze leaned over, plucking up my dad's old shotgun. "What's this for?"

"I was the first one here. Brittany told me that Garrett was in some kind of crisis, I don't know. Hindsight, it doesn't make much sense. It was just in case I needed to scare someone, I don't know. I haven't really been thinking that clear."

But nearly being murdered fixed that right up.

"There's not even anything in the chamber," Blaze raised a brow at me.

"It was Brittany..." Sheriff Myers muttered, turning

back around to where EMS personnel were loading her onto a stretcher. "Unbelievable." He headed back in that direction, his head hung low.

I took a deep breath and then let out a sharp exhale. "I guess you never really know someone."

"Nah, you never really do," Blaze grunted, his eyes still focused on the shotgun. "We've all got our shit though, I guess it's just how you choose to move past it."

"I suppose so," I said mindlessly as my eyes drifted back to Garrett, who was now speaking to his father. The ambulance with Brittany was already leaving, and as it zoomed past, I caught sight of the U.S. Marshal, who was apparently still lurking around the town. "Are you ever gonna tell me what he's here for?" I asked, turning back to Blaze.

"Who? Daniel?" He glanced over to the Marshal. "I thought I already told you he's on a serial killer hunt. Though by the looks of it, I don't think he's doing too well. He might need to up his game." Blaze chuckled, shaking his head. "He's just gonna end up getting sucked into all the small town drama."

As if he could hear us talking about him, the Marshal turned, and headed right for us. "Beth Young?" he asked as he approached, sticking out his hand. "Daniel Marlow, U.S. Marshal."

"Yeah, I can read the big letters on the back of your shirt," I quipped, shaking his hand. "But it's nice to meet you."

"Right back at ya. You think we could talk for a few moments? Alone?" he added, eyeing Blaze.

"Sure," I said with shrug.

"I'll take this as my cue to leave," Blaze huffed, heading off toward Sheriff Myers.

"What can I do for you?" I turned my attention to the Marshal.

"Well, I heard through the grapevine that you saw a dark colored truck coming down this road a few days ago—could you tell me what make or model it was by chance?"

How does he know about that?

I glanced over to Blaze, who was the only one who knew, before turning back. "I don't really know. I think it was a Dodge half-ton though."

Daniel's lip twitched, but that was the only reaction he had. "What time do you think that was?"

"I don't know, maybe eight-thirty or so?" I tried to recall that night. "They were creeping pretty slow through here. Then they blinded me with their brights."

"You're a lucky woman," he muttered, shaking his head. "Stay off the back roads at night, Miss Young. A high-profile criminal is in the area, and I hate to admit it, but the guy has always been a couple steps ahead of me."

"Oh," I said, my voice wavering slightly. "I'll keep that in mind."

As if not avoiding being murdered twice is some sort of stroke of luck.

"Keep your head up, Beth." He gave me a partial smile. "Word is you're a damn good lawyer, and I heard there's a need for a defender in the area. You might consider putting down some roots. Not that I'd be happy about it. I don't wanna go up against someone like you."

"You're too kind," I joked. "But yeah, I might just put down some roots... right here in Rustdale."

EPILOGUE

Eight months later...

I pulled up to the rehab facility, seeing Garrett already standing outside with his bag slung over his shoulder. I chuckled at the sight, not surprised that he was dying to get out of the place. He had sworn that he was never taking another drink again once he found out about Brittany being a murderer, but still had taken the advice from Mom and me to go through a treatment program. Besides, Brittany was still writing him letters from federal prison...

And that had to be annoying.

"Hey," Garrett greeted me as he opened the door of my truck. "You ever gonna retire this old thing?"

"Nah," I patted the dash. "I'll probably just put a new motor in her or something."

"You could just buy a new truck and save this one for occasional use." Garrett tossed his bag into the backseat. "It's not like you wouldn't drive it ever."

"You came out of rehab to be a life coach, huh?" I raised my brow at him.

He chuckled, rolling his eyes. "Ah, and you only get sassier by the day, Beth."

"Yeah, well, you know." I shrugged. "Mom has some massive dinner planned for tonight by the way."

"Doesn't she always?" He eyed me. "Every time you visited me, you said the same thing."

"Well, I mean, that's just her thing now."

"Like you don't enjoy those cooking classes, too?" he teased, his eyes clear and sparkling as he looked over at me.

I pulled out of the parking lot, thankful it was the last time I would ever make the forty-five-minute drive to the facility for Garrett. I was driving the wheels right off the old truck, seeing him three times a week. I felt my mouth grow dry as I turned onto the highway, heading back to Rustdale. I stole another glance over at him, feeling some kind of way that I couldn't define.

Well, I could. I just wasn't ready to admit it to him yet.

He leaned back in the seat, closing his eyes and taking a deep breath. "I have been waiting ages to get out of that hell hole."

"Yeah, me, too. This fuel expense is killing me."

Garrett opened one eye at me. "No one asked you to drive a million miles a week to bug me. Didn't even have enough time to make you a new macaroni necklace before you'd be showing up again. Flattering, really."

"Shut up," I laughed, swatting his arm. "It was a good distraction."

"From your new case?" he asked, suddenly growing serious and sitting up straight.

"Yeah, something like that," I said, pursing my lips.

"Is it your mom's relentless matchmaking then?" He couldn't hide his smile, and I hated the way it stirred something in my chest—something so much deeper than I had ever intended.

"She's kind of given up on that." My voice was careful as I brushed some of my hair out of my face. "I think she knows I'm not really looking."

"Hmm," was all he said, though I could see the smile forming on his face. "That's good to know."

"Yeah, why is that?"

"I don't know. I guess it just means I need to get all my shit together before I'll impress you enough to start looking."

I laughed, shaking my head. "Garrett."

"Yeah, well I got a job all lined up if that counts for something. I guess we'll see how it goes working with my old man. I might kill him or, more like, he kills me."

"Nah, he won't be that bad to work with. He hasn't shut up about you starting tomorrow. I've avoided Mary's Café for that sole reason. I swear that is *all* he talks about. I have to hear it on Sundays enough as it is."

"Ah, yeah, Beth Young, the proper church going

woman these days." He started laughing, his deep, clear voice louder than the engine of my dad's old truck. However, the laughter faded as he reached over, his hand landing on mine. I turned to look at him as he spoke, a jitter of excitement running up my arm. "Your dad would be really proud of what you've accomplished…and so would Sam. You've turned the ranch around and you and your mom are closer than ever. Life is good."

"Thanks, I know they'd both be so proud of you, too."

We both smiled at each other, something growing between us that I knew was the foundation of our future. Something would make my mom very happy.

Well, and me, too.

Here I was with new beginnings in the town I could no longer imagine leaving.

Rustdale, Texas.

WANT MORE?

Access a bonus short story told through the eyes of Sarah the night she went missing. Follow the link below to get your free story!

www.latigopress.com/bonus-content

Also, Andi's second book, The Back Road Phantom: A Cross Country Serial Killer, is out for preorder. You can find it here.

All the best,

Latigo Press, LLC

ABOUT THE AUTHOR

Andi Warden

With a love for crime and romance, Andi has always thought there's nothing better than a mixture of the two. She grew up in a small town in Oklahoma, and so when you pick up one of her books, you'll find yourself immersed in a world influenced by her experiences.

When she's not writing, you'll find her spending her days with her family and animals--or immersed in a true crime podcast.

BOOKS BY THIS AUTHOR

The Back Road Phantom: A Cross Country Serial Killer

Curious about the serial killer haunting the back roads of Texas? Prepare for the hunt of a lifetime through the eyes of none other than Daniel Marlow, the U.S. Marshal introduced in Everyone's Sweetheart.

Made in the USA
Middletown, DE
06 June 2023